U0010698

絕望的刀刺進了我的青春

OSCAR WILDE

王爾德——著   張家綺——譯
Oscar Wilde

目錄

－ 詩人王爾德：反骨的英國性 －

台大外文系教授 高維泓

　　在二十一世紀談王爾德（1854-1900），閃過眾人腦海無非是他的兩個身分，一是文學家，以刻劃英國上流社會虛偽的劇作與小說出名，二是同／雙性戀的身分。前者的成就無庸置疑，後者卻讓王爾德萬劫不復，從當紅文學才子變成過街老鼠。一八九五年，正當王爾德名望如日中天，同時有兩齣戲在倫敦劇院熱鬧上演[1]，他的同性愛人道格拉斯（Lord Alfred Douglas）的父親控訴他違反「性悖軌法[2]」（Sodomy law）。在媒體喧騰與法官濫權下，王爾德被視為異端，判監禁並服苦役兩年，所有財物遭拍賣一空。出獄後的王爾德已是社會棄兒，只得靠朋友接濟，隱姓埋名移居巴黎，三年後孤獨地於某旅館與世長辭。直到一九五四年，亦是王爾德受審的六十年後，曾參與當年審判的英國法官亨福芮斯爵士（Sir Travers Humphreys）才為他平反：「當年根本就不應該起訴王爾德。[3]」同年倫敦郡議會為了紀念他的百歲冥誕，於他住過的泰德街故居設了一個紀念牌。然而，當年的「恐同」早已摧毀一個超凡拔俗的作家。

　　這遲來的平反為同性戀平權運動史畫下新的一頁，但在文學史上，王爾德的詩藝直到今天都尚未獲得公允的評價。很少人關注當年猶是文青時期的他，踏入文壇的「起手式」是詩，離世前也是以長詩〈瑞丁監獄之歌〉（The Ballad of Reading Gaol）向糟蹋他的凡夫俗子告別。他甚至認為一八九三年發表的詩劇《莎樂美》（Salomé）比觀眾喜愛的其他舞台劇都好。他曾要求詩集出版社在合約及廣告裡，只能以「詩人」來稱呼他，而非「作者」。可見他十分嚴肅看待詩人這個身分。

　　要評價王爾德的詩，不能不提原生家庭的影響。他的父

親是位外科醫生，母親珍・王爾德（Lady Jane Wilde, 1821-1896）除了熱中蒐集與翻譯本土民間故事，也是支持愛爾蘭民族主義及維護女權的詩人。她所發表的激進政論〈木已成舟〉（The Die is Cast），因鼓吹顛覆英國統治，導致雜誌遭政府查禁。王爾德在這樣的家庭長大，比一般愛爾蘭人更直接地接觸反英國統治的種種訊息。母親的詩人及女性主義者身分，除了啟發他在文學與美學的品味與愛好，也使他習於用批判性的觀點戲謔偽善或不公義的社會現象。

王爾德在都柏林三一學院（Trinity College）及牛津大學就讀期間，所寫的英語詩即散見於愛爾蘭刊物。在他一八八一年出版第一本詩選《Poems》之前，他已經發表至少四十首詩，包括一八七八年獲得牛津大學紐帝蓋特獎（Newdigate Prize）的詩作〈拉溫納〉（Ravenna）。在此之前，詩情洋溢的他已有四首作品被收入愛爾蘭詩選《Lyra Hibernica Sacra》中[4]。值得玩味的是，即使已經負笈英國念書，大多數收錄在《Poems》裡的詩作，反而是先刊登於愛爾蘭本地的刊物，可見文青王爾德當時對於獲得出生地讀者肯定的渴望，似乎遠高於獲得英國本地讀者的認同。不幸的是，《Poems》出版後，在英國多招致負評：「王爾德先生的詩也許很美，但缺乏原創性，可以看到許多作家的影子。」批評家甚至不願意給王爾德任何讚賞，一方面批評他的詩「薄弱」，同時又說他的詩有六十幾位名作家的影子，例如莎士比亞（William Shakespeare）、希尼（Philip Sidney）、東恩（John Donne）、拜倫（Lord Byron）、莫里斯（William Morris）等等[5]。持平而論，即便這些詩是王爾德年輕時學習寫詩的仿作，能被批評家指出有經典作家的影子，很難說不是貶中帶褒，或是要挫挫這位來自愛爾蘭年輕新秀的銳氣。然而，批評家當年把還是詩壇小咖的王爾德與前輩大咖相比，似乎沒能預見在不久的將來，他將與這些文壇經典作家平起平坐[6]。

儘管王爾德早年的詩作多在愛爾蘭出版，當代評者認為他在牛津大學念書那些年（1874-1879），是他褪除「愛爾蘭味」（Irish intonation），詩風轉為「穩重且特殊的英國風」的時期[7]，詩人甚至自承，他連口音都改變了[8]。這種自我改造，無論是有意或無意，都反應在他的詩作裡。舉〈濟慈之墳〉（The Grave of Keats）為例，這首詩表現對英國浪漫主義詩人濟慈的崇拜[9]。濟慈筆下的抒情田園風，呼應了文青王爾德所追尋的美學內涵。儘管王爾德與因肺結核英年早逝於羅馬的濟慈非屬同一世代，他仍憧憬自己能有濟慈的詩風，透露出**我們**都是「大英母國的詩人畫家」：

> 噢，為不幸而碎的驕傲之心！
> 噢，米蒂利尼後最甜美的唇！
> 噢，咱大英母國的詩人畫家！
> 你的名寫在海水裡──應當永存：
> 我的眼淚將永保你的記憶長青，
> 一如伊莎貝拉所栽植的羅勒樹。

　　王爾德在一八七九年之後創作的詩，少有以愛爾蘭為描繪對象，而多著墨英國讀者感興趣的題目[10]。若從泛政治的角度檢視王爾德的選材，詩人為打入英國核心詩壇，有計畫地讓作品比英國人還英國，刻意凸顯繼承英國文化與美學的精髓。這種轉變讓後世評者無法用二分法來判定王爾德究竟是「哈英」還是「哈愛」，是英國還是愛爾蘭作家。儘管詩人出身愛爾蘭民族主義家庭，但做為唯美主義（aestheticism）的信徒，寫詩不是為政治服務，而是忠於內心對異文化的包容與孺慕，並非否定愛爾蘭文化的價值。若要給王爾德硬扣上背離愛爾蘭獨立運動的帽子，都會陷入政治陷阱或畫地自限的謬誤。

　　值得注意的是，王爾德並非對帝國的一切照單全收。儘

管詩作如〈為女皇歡呼〉（Ave Imperatrix）及〈自由的聖潔飢荒〉（Libertatis Sacra Fames）表達了身為日不落國一員的驕傲、對英國充分掌握海權的讚賞，甚至對英國文明與君主立憲體制的推崇，卻在字裡行間顯露出，他反對軍國主義及對異文化的侵犯掠奪。在〈為女皇歡呼〉裡，前半段歌詠帝國的興盛，後半段卻鉅細靡遺描繪戰爭的可怖，以及死無葬身之地的悲慘。從王爾德的觀點，大英帝國以眾多無辜青年死亡為代價，卻不容許人質疑其正當性：

> 英勇強壯敏捷的人上哪去？
> 英格蘭的騎士精神上哪去？
> 野草就是他們的裹屍布，
> 啜泣海浪則是他們的輓歌。
>
> 噢，躺臥於遙遠他鄉的摯愛，
> 死亡之唇豈能傳遞愛的絮語！
> 噢，荒蕪的飛塵！噢，無知的泥土！
> 難道這就是終點！難道這就是終點！

　　簡言之，王爾德不反對帝國主義，但反對以拓展與鞏固海外領土為名，行壓榨之實的軍國主義[11]。這個態度並未與他從小在家中耳濡目染的愛爾蘭民族主義相矛盾。對他而言，愛爾蘭受英國統治並非沒有好處，但訴諸暴力來取得國家或種族利益，畢竟不值得歌功頌德。

　　文青王爾德為追求夢想，勇於離開舒適圈，從都柏林到牛津念書，再從牛津到倫敦發展。這使他從區域性的作家，歷經了英國菁英文化的洗禮，體驗日不落國傳達給英格蘭人的優越感，並洞悉帝國假共榮真暴力的真相。對於一個敏感早慧的詩人而言，離開家鄉後的這些經歷與刺激，必然劇烈衝擊了其智識與心靈；內心的疑惑、身分的認同、情感的移

轉都顯示在詩風的轉變、選取的主題，甚至所投稿的雜誌。換言之，閱讀與研究王爾德的詩，未必需要探究是否仿作前輩（這對於正在學寫詩的人再正常不過），而是詩人如何透過書寫傳達內心的焦慮與渴望，翻轉或打破原有的意識框架，成為更精進的創作者。

究竟如何評價王爾德的詩藝，至今仍無定論，但如果回到當年他出版《Poems》的時空，反倒是大西洋彼岸的美國評論家，對他的詩抱有高度肯定。紐約時報就稱：「英格蘭有了新詩人……王爾德是繼丁尼生（Lord Alfred Tennyson）之後的桂冠詩人。[12]」評者更舉〈為女皇歡呼〉為例，認為該詩在美學上是英國風（Englishness）的代表，更是整部詩集最好的一首；王爾德之所以無法在英國得到公允評價，乃因「他的環境有著不健康的文學與社會氛圍[13]」。大西洋兩岸對王爾德詩藝的兩極回應，有可能是因為政治與地理距離差異，產生不同的美感，但美國讀者或許更能「就詩論詩」來客觀評賞詩人的作品。

在英語做為帝國強勢語言的情境下，王爾德的確趁此浪頭，將自己打造成高度英國化（Anglicization）的品牌，不僅便於容身保守且自傲的島國文壇，並用此身分於一八八一年到美國七十多個城鎮巡迴演講。無論被吹捧或貶低，他不曾遺忘自己是愛爾蘭人。一八八二年四月當他抵達舊金山，面對著幾乎全是愛爾蘭裔的聽眾，他的講題就是「愛爾蘭詩人與十九世紀的詩」，談及了當時英愛政治間的緊繃關係。根據當地報導，當天王爾德的演講「激發愛爾蘭人及其孩子們的國族感情[14]」。他的英愛雙重身分，對身為英語創作者的他無疑是一大利多，但內心對愛爾蘭局勢的關切，將他與同樣離鄉背井的同胞緊緊聯繫在一起。

在美國巡迴演講時，王爾德曾說：「保持清醒的首要條件就是跟四分之三的英國人都意見相左」。他與生俱來的反骨性格見證了大起大落的一生；在創作方面，無論是透過

喜劇諷刺英國上流社會的虛偽矯作，或是生前最後一首長詩〈瑞丁監獄之歌〉，都是用不同方式表達對傳統階級社會踐踏人性尊嚴的不滿。

王爾德的詩有個人獨特的美學品味，時而獨白，時而深入社會敏感議題，與他的劇作和小說一樣充滿力量與悲憫，卻鮮少被仔細研究或介紹，遑論翻譯。想了解王爾德如何從愛爾蘭民族主義者之子，躋身牛津與倫敦菁英社群，以迄成為階下囚，最後抑鬱／異域而終，他的心路歷程就在這本新譯的《絕望的刀刺進了我的青春：王爾德詩選 I》裡。

1　這兩部戲分別是《理想丈夫》與《不可兒戲》。在此之前，王爾德已發表兩齣喜劇《溫夫人的扇子》與《無足輕重的女人》，都十分受觀眾歡迎。

2　當時尚未有同性戀這個概念。

3　詳見 Holland, Vyvan. *Oscar Wilde and His World*. London, Thames and Hudson, 1960. 126. Holland 為王爾德的次子。王爾德入獄之後，妻子和兩個兒子都改姓 Holland。王爾德出獄後以 Sebastian Melmoth 為名隱居法國。

4　這四首詩分別是〈O Well for him〉、〈The Unvintageable Sea〉、〈Onto One Dead〉、〈Day, Come not Thus〉。經更訂後後即為〈哭泣吧，慟，願善戰勝〉、〈新生〉、〈真知〉，及收錄於《王爾德詩選II》的〈西斯汀教堂響起的最後審判讚美詩〉。
　　該詩集由愛爾蘭出版社M'Caw發行。有趣的是，其中也收錄了王爾德母親的詩作〈Broken Chorus〉及〈Aspirations for Death〉。母子作品同在一個詩選裡，頗有傳承的意味。

5　詳見 Kohl, Norbert. *Oscar Wilde: The Works of a Conformist Rebel*. Cambridge: Cambridge University Press, 1989. 15-18.

6　倒是當時美國的文藝批評家十分欣賞王爾德詩作，不像英國人如此刻薄。這可能是因為脫離了殖民統治的社會氛圍，能更持平地欣賞詩人欲傳達的美學。

7　詳見 Ellman, Richard. *Oscar Wilde*. London: Vintage. 38.

8　在牛津念書的五年，他刻意讓發音更像英國人。在某次受邀朗誦愛爾蘭詩的場合，他自承：「我希望我有個適當的愛爾蘭口音來讀詩，但在牛津的日子讓我忘掉了這個口音。」見 Depper, Robert D. ed. *Oscar Wilde: Irish Poets and Poetry of the Nineteenth Century*. San Francisco: The Book Club of California. 31.

9　王爾德將個人浪漫主義風格的詩，收於《Poems》的〈Wind Flowers〉及〈Flowers of Gold〉兩個單元之中。有學者認為，這部選集呈現了濟慈、雪萊（Percy Bysshe Shelley）與華茲渥斯（William Wordsworth）的共同特色。

10　另一方面，為了讓英國詩壇接受，熱愛劇院的王爾德也為許多女演員寫頌揚詩。一八七九年他遷居倫敦，短短四個月就完成了相關主題的詩，並發表在當時普羅大眾閱讀的流行雜誌，於劇場圈內廣為流傳。有趣的是，這些頌揚詩未必跟女演員有直接關係，而是與她們所扮演的角色有關。在《Poems》選集中，這些詩被收入〈Impressions de Théâtre〉單元。

11　在〈時間的征服者〉（The Conqueror of Time）中，王爾德預測英帝國的衰退以及後殖民的情境。該詩亦收錄在《Poems》選集裡。

12　*The New York Times*, 1881 年 8 月 14 日，頁 10。

13　出處同上。許多英國學者引用舊時的批評，概括認為王爾德的詩沒有比前人好，卻迴避承認他能比英國人寫出更具英國味的詩，甚至更有歐洲風情或是歷史深度的詩作。

14　*The Examiner* (San Francisco), 1882 年 4 月 6 日。摘自 Frankel, Nick. " 'Ave Imperatrix': Oscar Wilde and the Poetry of Englishness." *Victorian Poetry*, 33.2（1997）. 133.

陌生人的淚水將為他填滿
那破碎已久、名為憐憫的甕，
只因哀悼他的人皆放逐者，
而放逐者永遠哀悼。

——王爾德墓誌銘，節自〈瑞丁監獄之歌〉

And alien tears will fill for him
Pity's long-broken urn,
For his mourner will be outcast men,
And outcasts always mourn.

——*The epitaph on Wilde's tomb, excerption from 'The Ballad of Reading Gaol'*

– From Spring Days to Winter –

In the glad springtime when leaves were green,
O merrily the throstle sings!
I sought, amid the tangled sheen,
Love whom mine eyes had never seen,
O the glad dove has golden wings!

Between the blossoms red and white,
O merrily the throstle sings!
My love first came into my sight,
O perfect vision of delight,
O the glad dove has golden wings!

The yellow apples glowed like fire,
O merrily the throstle sings!
O Love too great for lip or lyre,
Blown rose of love and of desire,
O the glad dove has golden wings!

But now with snow the tree is grey,
Ah, sadly now the throstle sings!
My love is dead: ah! well-a-day,
See at her silent feet I lay
A dove with broken wings!
Ah, Love! ah, Love! that thou wert slain—
Fond Dove, fond Dove return again!

– 春日轉冬 –

綠葉青翠的美好春季，
噢，畫眉鳥歡欣高歌！
我在盤繞錯綜的燦爛裡，
為雙眼不曾見的愛情尋覓，
噢，金色羽翼的快樂白鴿！

盛開花朵，紅白交織，
噢，畫眉鳥歡欣高歌！
我的愛情初次躍入了雙眼，
噢，完美愉悅的景致，
噢，金色羽翼的快樂白鴿！

澄黃蘋果猶如烈火閃亮，
噢，畫眉鳥歡欣高歌！
噢，愛情偉大無以歌唱，
愛與欲的玫瑰吹拂綻放，
噢，金色羽翼的快樂白鴿！

如今白雪靄靄，枯樹灰白，
啊，畫眉鳥淒淒哭啼！
我的愛已歿，嗚呼哀哉！
望見她腳邊，不語靜待，
是那白鴿折翼！
啊，愛啊！愛！已不再──
可愛白鴿，我可愛的鴿，求你歸來！

– Requiescat –

Tread lightly, she is near
Under the snow,
Speak gently, she can hear
The daisies grow.

All her bright golden hair
Tarnished with rust,
She that was young and fair
Fallen to dust.

Lily-like, white as snow,
She hardly knew
She was a woman, so
Sweetly she grew.

Coffin-board, heavy stone,
Lie on her breast,
I vex my heart alone
She is at rest.

Peace, Peace, she cannot hear
Lyre or sonnet,
All my life's buried here,
Heap earth upon it.

Avignon

－ 安魂賦 －

腳步放輕，她在身邊
瑞雪深埋，
語調柔緩，她可聽見
雛菊盛開。

她的金黃豔髮
經鐵鏽玷汙，
年輕貌美的她
卻凋落塵土。

白如瑞雪，恍如百合，
她一無所知
她已是女人，出落得
絕美標緻。

棺木與沉碑，
緊壓她胸前，
我暗自傷悲，
她幽幽永眠。

安息吧，安息，她再聽不見
詩歌或琴聲，
我的人生亦隨她安葬，
塵土埋我身。

亞維儂[1]

1　王爾德的十歲妹妹逝世七年後，他在法國亞維儂寫下此詩。王爾德經常造訪她的墳墓，
　　從中獲得平靜與慰藉。

– The Dole of the King's Daughter –

Seven stars in the still water,
And seven in the sky;
Seven sins on the King's daughter,
Deep in her soul to lie.

Red roses are at her feet,
(Roses are red in her red-gold hair)
And O where her bosom and girdle meet
Red roses are hidden there.

Fair is the knight who lieth slain
Amid the rush and reed,
See the lean fishes that are fain
Upon dead men to feed.

Sweet is the page that lieth there,
(Cloth of gold is goodly prey,)
See the black ravens in the air,
Black, O black as the night are they.

What do they there so stark and dead?
(There is blood upon her hand.)
Why are the lilies flecked with red?
(There is blood on the river sand.)

There are two that ride from the south and east,
And two from the north and west,

– 國王之女的哀愁 –

靜謐止水映著七顆星，
天空裡高掛著七顆星；
國王之女犯了七宗罪，
深深鎖在她的靈魂內。

豔紅玫瑰歇在她的腳邊，
（在她緋金髮梢間嬌緋）
噢，她的胸膛與腰帶間
收藏著一朵朵朱紅玫瑰。

殞落的騎士多麼俊美
躺在燈草與蘆葦之間，
瞧那瘦扁小魚兒欣喜
逝去男人今可當餐飯。

侍從倒在那兒，模樣可愛，
（金線衣是美好獵物，）
瞧那穹蒼飛翔的漆黑渡鴉，
噢，牠們黝黑，黑如深夜。

他們怎在那兒僵冷長眠？
（她手上沾染鮮血。）
百合花兒何來斑斑紅點？
（河沙上血跡斑斑。）

兩人從東南方騎馬而來，
還有兩人自西北方而來，

For the black raven a goodly feast,
For the King's daughter rest.

There is one man who loves her true,
(Red, O red, is the stain of gore!)
He hath duggen a grave by the darksome yew,
(One grave will do for four.)

No moon in the still heaven,
In the black water none,
The sins on her soul are seven,
The sin upon his is one.

對於渡鴉，是絕好宴席，
國王之女，則永恆安息。

有一個人，真心愛著她，
（噢，豔紅是血跡的紅！）
幽暗邪惡紫杉旁掘了墳，
（一片墓地，四命共葬。）

靜默天國不見月色，
黑水不見月影映照，
她靈魂裡藏著七條罪惡，
為他犯的罪是其中之一。

〈月亮裡的女人 The Woman in the Moon〉
一般認為，比亞茲萊畫的月中人臉即是王爾德。

– 哭泣吧，慟，願善戰勝 –

噢，安居樂業可好，
在領地裡穿金戴銀，
毋需擔心滂沱大雨，
不必憂愁林木塌倒。

噢，不知真相可好，
不識飢荒歲月苦痛，
不曉蒼髮老父悲與淚，
不知母親正暗自垂淚。

但，踏遍道路才是好，
走過勞倦折磨與掙扎，
卻從生命的沉痛點滴，
築出貼近上帝的階梯。

– Cry woe, woe, and let the good prevail[1] –

O well for him who lives at ease
With garnered gold in wide domain,
Nor heeds the splashing of the rain,
The crashing down of forest trees.

1　原標題為古希臘文 Αἴλινον, αἴλινον εἰπέ τὸ δεὐ νιχάτω。

O well for him who ne'er hath known
The travail of the hungry years,
A father grey with grief and tears,
A mother weeping all alone.

But well for him whose foot hath trod
The weary road of toil and strife,
Yet from the sorrows of his life
Builds ladders to be nearer God.

〈孔雀裙 The Peacock Skirt〉
猶太公主莎樂美，在王爾德筆下的形象既危險又性感。

– The True Knowledge –

Thou knowest all; I seek in vain
What lands to till or sow with seed—
The land is black with briar and weed,
Nor cares for falling tears or rain.

Thou knowest all; I sit and wait
With blinded eyes and hands that fail,
Till the last lifting of the veil
And the first opening of the gate.

Thou knowest all; I cannot see.
I trust I shall not live in vain,
I know that we shall meet again
In some divine eternity.

– 真知 –

你全局知悉；我徒勞無功，
不知哪塊土地需播種翻耕——
土壤荊棘遍布，野草焦黑，
不在乎從天而降的雨或淚。

你全局知悉；我坐等空待，
雙眼盲然，手腳無用，
直至最終面紗揭開，
直至大門初次敞開。

你全局知悉；我目不可視。
我相信我並未白活一生，
我知道我們將再度重逢，
來日，在某個神聖永恆。

– A Vision –

Two crowned Kings, and One that stood alone
With no green weight of laurels round his head,
But with sad eyes as one uncomforted,
And wearied with man's never-ceasing moan
For sins no bleating victim can atone,
And sweet long lips with tears and kisses fed.
Girt was he in a garment black and red,
And at his feet I marked a broken stone
Which sent up lilies, dove-like, to his knees.
Now at their sight, my heart being lit with flame,
I cried to Beatrice, 'Who are these?'
And she made answer, knowing well each name,
'Æschylos first, the second Sophokles,
And last (wide stream of tears!) Euripides.'

- 幻象 -

兩名加冠國王，還有一位遺世獨立，
頭頂無詩人桂冠的青翠重量，
眼底卻堆滿未得撫慰的惆悵，
為人類無法揮別的哀號倦疲，
代罪羔羊都無法洗刷的罪惡，
甜美渴望雙唇，淚水和吻餵養。
披掛紅黑衣裳的他堅忍不拔，
在他腳邊瞥見一顆破裂碎石，
石縫蹦出百合[1]，恍若白鴿，升騰至膝。
目睹一切，我心燃火苗，
哭喊著問貝緹麗彩[2]，「他們是何人？」
她聞聲應答，如數家珍，
「第一位是埃斯庫羅斯，第二位索福克勒斯，
最後（淚水止不住潰堤！），是歐里庇得斯[3]。」

---

1 據傳聖母瑪利亞摘下黃百合後顏色轉白，此後百合又名聖母之花，因此歐洲中世紀起，
   百合即為聖潔象徵。
2 貝緹麗彩是但丁的戀人，早逝的她成為但丁的繆思，在《神曲》中擔任地獄嚮導。
3 分別為希臘三大悲劇詩人。

– Sonnet on Approaching Italy –

I reached the Alps: the soul within me burned
Italia, my Italia, at thy name:
And when from out the mountain's heart I came
And saw the land for which my life had yearned,
I laughed as one who some great prize had earned:
And musing on the story of thy fame
I watched the day, till marked with wounds of flame
The turquoise sky to burnished gold was turned,
The pine-trees waved as waves a woman's hair,
And in the orchards every twining spray
Was breaking into flakes of blossoming foam:
But when I knew that far away at Rome
In evil bonds a second Peter lay,
I wept to see the land so very fair.

Turin

– 臨近義大利之歌 –

我抵達阿爾卑斯山：你的名點燃我內心的靈魂，
義大利，我的義大利：
我自山的心臟而來
瞥見我畢生渴望的國土，
彷彿贏得大獎，笑咧了嘴：
咀嚼著你的名，你的故事，
這天我凝視你，直至烈焰刻下傷，
土耳其藍天空，亦染上光澤金黃。
松樹波浪彎曲如女人髮絲，
果園裡的枝椏，雙雙對對
裂成開花盛放的瓣瓣碎沫：
然當我得知，在遠方羅馬
第二個彼得[1]面臨邪惡桎梏，
透過淚眼看著這國土的美。

都靈

---

1   彼得是耶穌十二門徒之首，遭羅馬皇帝尼祿處決，殉道而亡。王爾德的夢想是有生之
     年探訪義大利，參見教宗。滿心盼望此行之時寫出此詩。當時教宗比約九世不承認義
     大利國王伊曼紐二世建立的王國，遭褫奪教會領土，形同桎梏。王爾德將他描寫為「第
     二個彼得」。

– Sonnet Written in Holy Week at Genoa –

I wandered in Scoglietto's far retreat,
The oranges on each o'erhanging spray
Burned as bright lamps of gold to shame the day;
Some startled bird with fluttering wings and fleet
Made snow of all the blossoms; at my feet
Like silver moons the pale narcissi lay:
And the curved waves that streaked the great green bay
Laughed i' the sun, and life seemed very sweet.
Outside the young boy-priest passed singing clear,
Jesus the Son of Mary has been slain,
O come and fill His sepulchre with flowers.
Ah, God! Ah, God! those dear Hellenic hours
Had drowned all memory of Thy bitter pain,
The Cross, the Crown, the Soldiers, and the Spear.

– 筆於熱那亞的聖週 [1] –

我漫步在史柯格列朵 [2] 的遙遠偏鄉，
高聳枝椏上的柳橙
恍若金色明燈灼燒，白晝失色；
驚弓之鳥拍振雙翅，紛飛逃竄
綻放花瓣雪片紛落；我的腳邊
靜躺著猶如銀月的蒼白水仙：
點綴著浩瀚綠灣的波浪卷卷
陽光底下輕笑，生命彷彿甜美。
外頭途經的年輕牧師歌喉清脆，
高聲唱著瑪利亞之子耶穌的死，
噢，來吧，在他墳邊擺滿花卉。
啊，上帝啊上帝！那些美好的希臘歲月
淹沒了祢所有的苦澀痛楚記憶，
十字架，皇冠，士兵，長矛，皆已消逝。

1　也作「受難週（Passion Week）」，復活節的前一週。
2　位於熱那亞東南方。

– The Theatre at Argos –

Nettles and poppy mar each rock-hewn seat:
No poet crowned with olive deathlessly
Chants his glad song, nor clamorous Tragedy
Startles the air; green corn is waving sweet
Where once the Chorus danced to measures fleet;
Far to the East a purple stretch of sea,
The cliffs of gold that prisoned Danae;
And desecrated Argos at my feet.

No season now to mourn the days of old,
A nation's shipwreck on the rocks of Time,
Or the dread storms of all-devouring Fate,
For now the peoples clamour at our gate,
The world is full of plague and sin and crime,
And God Himself is half-dethroned for Gold!

– 阿哥斯劇院 –

蕁麻和罌粟玷汙了岩石色澤的座椅：
頭戴不朽橄欖枝葉的桂冠詩人，無一
唱頌他的喜劇，抑無哭天搶地的悲劇
震撼空氣；青綠穀粒甜美地
在合唱團隨節奏起舞之地，波浪起伏；
遙遠東方，紫海綿延，
禁錮達妮[1]的金色懸崖；
在我腳邊褻瀆阿哥斯。

如今不再有哀悼舊時的季節，
國家沉船擱淺在時光的礁岩，
或是吞噬命運的恐怖暴風雨，
而今門外眾人喧譁騷然，
世界氾濫著天災惡行和罪孽，
上帝亦為黃金遺落半個王位。

1　希臘神話典故。阿哥斯王國的公主達妮，因父親阿克里修斯聽信神諭，相信達妮的兒
　　子未來會弒殺他，便將達妮鎖在高塔，然而宙斯卻瞥見美麗的公主，化身黃金雨，進
　　入高塔，達妮因此懷孕。

– The Grave of Keats –

Rid of the world's injustice, and his pain,
He rests at last beneath God's veil of blue:
Taken from life when life and love were new
The youngest of the martyrs here is lain,
Fair as Sebastian, and as early slain.
No cypress shades his grave, no funeral yew,
But gentle violets weeping with the dew
Weave on his bones an ever-blossoming chain.
O proudest heart that broke for misery!
O sweetest lips since those of Mitylene!
O poet-painter of our English Land!
Thy name was writ in water—it shall stand:
And tears like mine will keep thy memory green,
As Isabella did her Basil-tree.

- 濟慈[1] 之墳 -

褪去世界的不公義，及他的傷痛，
他終在上帝的湛藍面紗底下長眠：
生命與愛正盛時，辭去生命，
安息此地的殉道者最為年輕，
英年早逝，俊如賽巴斯提安[2]。
柏樹與喪禮紫杉遮蔽不了墳墓，
溫柔紫羅蘭與露水，哀慟悲鳴，
為他的骨編織永恆綻放的桎梏。
噢，為不幸而碎的驕傲之心！
噢，米蒂利尼[3] 後最甜美的唇！
噢，咱大英母國的詩人畫家！
你的名寫在海水裡——應當永存：
我的眼淚將永保你的記憶長青，
一如伊莎貝拉所栽植的羅勒樹[4]。

1　John Keats（1795-1821），英國浪漫主義詩人，因肺結核病逝羅馬。

2　基督教殉道聖人。

3　希臘萊斯博斯島的首府，古時該城的抒情詩名聞遐邇。

4　典故來自濟慈的《伊莎貝拉的羅勒花盆》，故事描述伊莎貝拉的兩名兄長殺了她的愛
　　人羅倫佐，死後羅倫佐託夢，伊莎貝拉找到他的遺體後，砍下頭顱並埋在羅勒盆栽裡，
　　天天澆水。直到哥哥發現她行徑詭異，偷走盆栽，才發現裡面裝著羅倫佐的頭，之後
　　哥哥逃離翡冷翠，伊莎貝拉也在不久後死去。

– Sonnet on the Massacre of the Christians in Bulgaria –

Christ, dost Thou live indeed? or are Thy bones
Still straitened in their rock-hewn sepulchre?
And was Thy Rising only dreamed by her
Whose love of Thee for all her sin atones?
For here the air is horrid with men's groans,
The priests who call upon Thy name are slain,
Dost Thou not hear the bitter wail of pain
From those whose children lie upon the stones?
Come down, O Son of God! incestuous gloom
Curtains the land, and through the starless night
Over Thy Cross a Crescent moon I see!
If Thou in very truth didst burst the tomb
Come down, O Son of Man! and show Thy might
Lest Mahomet be crowned instead of Thee!

– 保加利亞基督徒大屠殺之歌 –

基督，祢是否存在？
抑或祢的骨仍深鎖在石塊墳墓？
難道祢的復活只是愛著祢的她
赦免罪孽的一場夢？
空氣裡瀰漫著男人的驚悚呻吟，
呼著祢名的牧師難逃殺戮之命，
祢難道沒聽見酸楚的慟哭嚎啕
從石塊上死屍的父母嘴裡升起？
降臨吧，噢，上帝之子！亂倫的昏天暗地
籠罩著這塊土地，瀰漫穿透漆黑無星的夜
在祢的十字架上，我瞥見弦月！
若祢真從墳裡起身復活，
降臨吧，噢，人民之子！展現祢的力量
否則頭戴王冠的將是穆罕默德，不是祢！

– Easter Day –

The silver trumpets rang across the Dome:
The people knelt upon the ground with awe:
And borne upon the necks of men I saw,
Like some great God, the Holy Lord of Rome.
Priest-like, he wore a robe more white than foam,
And, king-like, swathed himself in royal red,
Three crowns of gold rose high upon his head:
In splendour and in light the Pope passed home.
My heart stole back across wide wastes of years
To One who wandered by a lonely sea,
And sought in vain for any place of rest:
'Foxes have holes, and every bird its nest,
I, only I, must wander wearily,
And bruise my feet, and drink wine salt with tears.'

- 復活節 -

銀色號角，響遍穹頂：
敬畏的人們雙膝跪地：
我越過他們頸項望見一張面孔，
羅馬神聖君主，猶如偉大上帝。
一襲衣袍白過泡沫，儼然牧師，
貴氣大紅加身，君王架勢，
頭上輝煌頂著黃金三重冠：
教皇耀眼光彩行經平房宅邸。
我心潛回徒然荒漠的歲歲年年，
想起在寂寥大海孤獨漫步的他，
枉然尋覓著安身之所：
「鳥兒歸巢，狐狸安窩，
唯我得拖著疲憊身軀浪跡天涯。
我的雙足青紫，痛飲酒鹽淚水。」

〈黑斗篷 The Black Cape〉
比亞茲萊的《莎樂美》插畫有濃厚的浮世繪風格，畫面刻意不配合劇中文字，自成一格。

– 義大利 –

義大利！你已殞落，軍隊浩浩蕩蕩
自北阿爾卑斯山，邁向西西里海洋，
戰矛錚錚，輝煌爍亮！
是！國破城毀，眾國依然封你為后，
只因城裡舉目皆金銀財寶，
你寶石藍的湖水傲然濤濤，
目不暇給的軍艦，在紅白綠旗幟下，
率領受盡風吹日曬的前鋒。

噢，美麗而堅強！噢，堅強而美麗，
可惜徒勞！南望飽受褻瀆的羅馬城，
坍塌著悼念著上帝塗抹聖膏的國王！
抬頭仰望天國！上帝允許此事發生？
不！火焰環繞的拉斐爾下凡，
應以傷痛之劍，懲罰掠奪者。

威尼斯

– Italia –

Italia! thou art fallen, though with sheen
Of battle-spears thy clamorous armies stride
From the north Alps to the Sicilian tide!
Ay! fallen, though the nations hail thee Queen
Because rich gold in every town is seen,
And on thy sapphire lake in tossing pride

Of wind-filled vans thy myriad galleys ride
Beneath one flag of red and white and green.

O Fair and Strong! O Strong and Fair in vain!
Look southward where Rome's desecrated town
Lies mourning for her God-anointed King!
Look heaven-ward! shall God allow this thing?
Nay! but some flame-girt Raphael shall come down,
And smite the Spoiler with the sword of pain.

Venice

〈柏拉圖式哀悼 The Platonic Lament〉
畫中死者為年輕敘利亞軍官，他因愛慕莎樂美而自刎。

– Vita Nuova[1] –

I stood by the unvintageable sea
Till the wet waves drenched face and hair with spray,
The long red fires of the dying day
Burned in the west; the wind piped drearily;
And to the land the clamorous gulls did flee:
'Alas!' I cried, 'my life is full of pain,
And who can garner fruit or golden grain,
From these waste fields which travail ceaselessly!'
My nets gaped wide with many a break and flaw
Nathless I threw them as my final cast
Into the sea, and waited for the end.
When lo! a sudden glory! and I saw
The argent splendour of white limbs ascend,
And in that joy forgot my tortured past.

– 新生 –

我站在酒紅然非紅酒的海水邊
直到濕冷海浪濺得我容髮浸透，
生命將盡之日，高聳鮮紅火焰
在西方燃燒；陰鬱的朔風獵獵；
嘈嘈海鷗逃逸岸邊：
我呼喊：「嗚呼！我的生命充滿傷痛，
誰能在這片荒蕪田野，
孜孜不倦，收穫甜美果實或黃金穀粒！」
我的漁網缺口破洞無數，裂縫綻開，
我卻朝大海，最後一拋，
等待著最終一秒。
看啊！突如其來的得勝！
我看見那亮白四肢升起的銀光絕景，
那一刻的愉悅，令我忘卻沉痛過往。

1　標題為義大利文，是但丁的詩集。

– E Tenebris[1] –

Come down, O Christ, and help me! reach thy hand,
For I am drowning in a stormier sea
Than Simon on thy lake of Galilee:
The wine of life is spilt upon the sand,
My heart is as some famine-murdered land,
Whence all good things have perished utterly,
And well I know my soul in Hell must lie
If I this night before God's throne should stand.
'He sleeps perchance, or rideth to the chase,
Like Baal, when his prophets howled that name
From morn to noon on Carmel's smitten height.'
Nay, peace, I shall behold before the night,
The feet of brass, the robe more white than flame,
The wounded hands, the weary human face.

– 走出黑暗 –

降臨吧，噢，基督，拯救我！伸出你的手，
我將沉淪淹沒在暴風襲擊之海，
風狂浪湧之惡，更勝西門的加利利湖[2]險境：
生命的葡萄酒平白灑在沙地，
我的心猶如饑荒荼毒的土地，
所有美好皆已化為烏有，
若我今晚要佇立於上帝王位面前，
我清楚瞭然，我的靈魂將於地獄安息。
「他或許入眠，或者猶如巴力神，
狂奔追逐，而他的先知從日出到月明
都在風吹雨打的迦密山，呼喊他的名[3]。」
不，安息吧，我會在夜晚降臨前，
凝視黃銅般的足，那比烈焰灼白的袍，
受傷的雙手，及疲憊的人類面孔。

---

1 標題為拉丁文。
2 聖經馬太福音的故事，耶穌門徒西門在暴風雨落入加利利湖，耶穌走過湖面拯救他。
3 同為聖經典故。《列王記上》裡，以利亞嘲諷一群事奉巴力神的信徒，說他們有難時，
　巴力神恐怕在忙碌或呼呼大睡。

– Quantum Mutata –

There was a time in Europe long ago
When no man died for freedom anywhere,
But England's lion leaping from its lair
Laid hands on the oppressor! it was so
While England could a great Republic show.
Witness the men of Piedmont, chiefest care
Of Cromwell, when with impotent despair
The Pontiff in his painted portico
Trembled before our stern ambassadors.
How comes it then that from such high estate
We have thus fallen, save that Luxury
With barren merchandise piles up the gate
Where nobler thoughts and deeds should enter by:
Else might we still be Milton's heritors.

－ 過往雲煙 －

久遠以前的歐洲
尚無人為自由亡，
英格蘭雄獅離巢
雙手反抗暴君！這便是
英格蘭偉大共和國的體現。
皮埃蒙特[1]人見證了，克倫威爾[2]的
心心念念，伴隨無能為力的絕望，
看著彩繪柱廊裡的羅馬主教
於面目嚴肅的使者前顫巍巍。
我們是怎麼從如此崇高地位
墜落今日局勢，僅穿金戴銀，
空洞物質，高疊於城門，
高尚思想善舉亦當領進門：
無愧為米爾頓[3]後嗣。

1　義大利西北部的地區，為十九世紀中葉義大利統一的跳板。
2　Oliver Cromwell（1599-1659），十七世紀的英國政治領袖，廢除英格蘭君主制，並征服
　　蘇格蘭及愛爾蘭，擔任三國護國公。
3　John Milton（1608-1674），十七世紀的英國詩人，著有《失樂園》，主張精神至上，是
　　人類永恆的追尋。

– To Milton –

Milton! I think thy spirit hath passed away
From these white cliffs, and high-embattled towers;
This gorgeous fiery-coloured world of ours
Seems fallen into ashes dull and grey,
And the age changed unto a mimic play
Wherein we waste our else too-crowded hours:
For all our pomp and pageantry and powers
We are but fit to delve the common clay,
Seeing this little isle on which we stand,
This England, this sea-lion of the sea,
By ignorant demagogues is held in fee,
Who love her not: Dear God! is this the land
Which bare a triple empire in her hand
When Cromwell spake the word Democracy!

- 獻給米爾頓 -

米爾頓！你的精神必然已逝，
自潔白懸崖，備戰高聳之塔；
火紅絢麗的世界殞落
成了黯淡炭灰的餘燼，
物換星移，淪落模仿劇，
人們徒然浪費倥傯光陰：
只為浮華虛浮權勢
落為平凡適得其所，
目睹我們站立這座小島，
這座英格蘭，海上之獅，
受當權的無知政客蠱惑，
他並不愛她：親愛上帝！這豈是
克倫威爾訴說民主之時
她手中公布的那三帝國[1]！

1　指英格蘭、蘇格蘭、愛爾蘭組成的聯邦國，在十七世紀克倫威爾的任期內成立。

– Wasted Days (from a Picture Painted by Miss V. T.) –

A fair slim boy not made for this world's pain
With hair of gold thick clustering round his ears,
And longing eyes half veiled by foolish tears
Like bluest water seen through mists of rain;
Pale cheeks whereon no kiss hath left its stain,
Red under-lip drawn in for fear of love,
And white throat whiter than the breast of dove —
Alas! Alas! If all should be in vain,
Corn-fields behind, and reapers all a-row
In weariest labour, toiling wearily
To no sweet sound of laughter, or of lute;
And careless of the crimson sunset-glow,
The boy still dreams, nor knows that night is night,
And in the night-time no man gathers fruit.

– 荒蕪歲月（V. T. 女士畫作）–

纖細美男不為世間苦痛，
金黃秀髮飽滿鬈曲耳畔，
痴愚淚水半掩渴望雙眼，
蔚藍海水透出繚繞雨霧；
蒼白面頰不留一絲吻痕，
懼怕愛情，緊咬紅潤下唇，
白皙喉頸的皓白更勝鴿胸──
嗚呼！嗚呼！萬事皆白費，
後方玉米田，收割人齊立，
含著淚，咬著牙，苦耕耘，
不聞甜蜜笑語與詩琴樂音；
男孩不顧猩紅熾熱的陽光，
依然美夢，卻不知夜已深，
亦不曉夜裡無人收穫果實。

– Theoretikos –

This mighty empire hath but feet of clay:
Of all its ancient chivalry and might
Our little island is forsaken quite:
Some enemy hath stolen its crown of bay,
And from its hills that voice hath passed away
Which spake of Freedom: O come out of it,
Come out of it, my Soul, thou art not fit
For this vile traffic-house, where day by day
Wisdom and reverence are sold at mart,
And the rude people rage with ignorant cries
Against an heritage of centuries.
It mars my calm: wherefore in dreams of Art
And loftiest culture I would stand apart,
Neither for God, nor for his enemies.

– 沉思冥想 –

雄偉帝國僅剩泥土雙足：
古老騎士精神與英勇中
吾家小島已遭到遺棄：
敵軍奪走了海灣榮冠，
山丘傳來之聲亦逝去，
那聲音曾訴說自由：噢，走吧，
走吧，我的靈魂，這幢非法屋
並不適合你住，日復一日
市集拍賣智慧崇敬，
粗俗之人對世紀傳承的遺產
發出無知怒吼。
我的冷靜毀滅：為何藝術與
崇高文化的美夢裡我必須勢不兩立，
既不為上帝，亦不為祂的敵人。

– Amor Intellectualis –

Oft have we trod the vales of Castaly
And heard sweet notes of sylvan music blown
From antique reeds to common folk unknown:
And often launched our bark upon that sea
Which the nine Muses hold in empery,
And ploughed free furrows through the wave and foam,
Nor spread reluctant sail for more safe home
Till we had freighted well our argosy.
Of which despoilèd treasures these remain,
Sordello's passion, and the honied line
Of young Endymion, lordly Tamburlaine
Driving his pampered jades, and more than these,
The seven-fold vision of the Florentine,
And grave-browed Milton's solemn harmonies.

– 以靈智愛神 [1] –

我們不時踏過卡斯塔里 [2] 山谷
聽聞甜美森林裡的樂音吹送
自古老蘆葦，傳至未知庶民：
亦不時向大海咆哮訴諸，
海域統治歸九位繆思女神，
海浪泡沫裡自由耕耘犁溝，
除非我們的貨船滿載而歸
莫不甘張帆，平安歸返。
掠奪寶物中，
還剩下索德羅 [3] 的熱情，
青春恩底彌翁的輪廓，而威嚴高傲的帖木兒
駕著他那備受寵愛的瘦馬，
亦有翡冷翠人的七層地獄，
以及米爾頓 [4] 眉宇深鎖的莊嚴和諧。

1　十七世紀荷蘭宗教哲學家史賓諾莎（Baruch Spinoza, 1632-1677）提出的概念，他相信上
　　帝與宇宙為一體，人類智慧則是上帝智慧所組成，上帝透過自然法則主宰世界，是物
　　質和精神世界的因，有其必然性，唯有認知這種必然，方可通往自由。

2　希臘神話裡，繆思女神的泉水所在地。

3　十三世紀的義大利吟遊詩人。

4　引述米爾頓《失樂園》，描寫人性的墮落與救贖，永恆的失去與復得。

〈約翰與莎樂美 John and Salom〉
莎樂美向施洗者約翰索求一吻。

－ 維洛納隨筆 －

國王宮殿的階梯陡峭，
我放逐疲倦的腳難熬，
噢，麵包是何等鹹澀，
碎屑從惡人餐桌墜落，──還是
在血腥戰役死去的好，
或頭顱高掛翡冷翠城門，
活出骨氣，都好過苟活，
任由消磨我靈魂的精髓。

「詛咒上帝，然後死去：還有比這更好的企望？
幸福的他早已忘卻你，
沉浸黃金國城，永恆之日」──
不，安息吧：盲目牢獄後方
我擁有的東西，無人帶得走，
有我的愛，和滿天星斗光芒。

－ At Verona －

How steep the stairs within Kings' houses are
For exile-wearied feet as mine to tread,
And O how salt and bitter is the bread
Which falls from this Hound's table,—better far
That I had died in the red ways of war,
Or that the gate of Florence bare my head,

Than to live thus, by all things comraded
Which seek the essence of my soul to mar.

'Curse God and die: what better hope than this?
He hath forgotten thee in all the bliss
Of his gold city, and eternal day'—
Nay peace: behind my prison's blinded bars
I do possess what none can take away,
My love, and all the glory of the stars.

〈希羅底登場 Enter Herodias〉
希羅底是莎樂美的母親,因與叔叔腓力結婚,後又改嫁希律王,而受施洗者約翰的指責。

– Athanasia[1] –

To that gaunt House of Art which lacks for naught
Of all the great things men have saved from Time,
The withered body of a girl was brought
Dead ere the world's glad youth had touched its prime,
And seen by lonely Arabs lying hid
In the dim womb of some black pyramid.

But when they had unloosed the linen band
Which swathed the Egyptian's body,— lo! was found
Closed in the wasted hollow of her hand
A little seed, which sown in English ground
Did wondrous snow of starry blossoms bear,
And spread rich odors through our springtide air.

With such strange arts this flower did allure
That all forgotten was the asphodel,
And the brown bee, the lily's paramour,
Forsook the cup where he was wont to dwell,
For not a thing of earth it seemed to be,
But stolen from some heavenly Arcady.

In vain the sad narcissus, wan and white
At its own beauty, hung across the stream,
The purple dragon-fly had no delight
With its gold-dust to make his wings a-gleam,
Ah! no delight the jasmine-bloom to kiss,
Or brush the rain-pearls from the eucharis.

– 埃塔娜西亞 –

荒涼的藝術殿堂無所匱乏，
人們世代流傳的宏偉盛大，
女孩凋零的軀體死亡衰敗，
人間志得意滿的青春尚未盛開，
孤單阿拉伯人發現她倒地不起
藏匿在烏黑金字塔的幽暗子宮。

然而就在他們鬆綁那包裹著
埃及遺體的亞麻繩時——看啊！
她文風不動的手掌緊緊握著
一顆小小種籽，耕種英國土壤
猶如滿天星斗盛開成斑斑白雪，
在滿潮的天空，飄散濃郁香氛。

花朵的詭譎攻心計謀
引誘人們遺忘長春花，
而褐色蜜蜂，百合的情夫，
則遺棄他安居舒適的花朵，
只因這似是竊自仙境阿卡迪，
而非大地人間之物。

淒淒水仙，徒勞慘白萎靡，
垂首溪水，獨自慕望美貌，
紫色蜻蜓不滿意自己
金黃粉塵的熠熠翅膀，
啊！一親芳澤盛開茉莉並不可喜，
掠過亞馬遜百合落下的雨珠亦然。

For love of it the passionate nightingale
Forgot the hills of Thrace, the cruel king,
And the pale dove no longer cared to sail
Through the wet woods at time of blossoming,
But round this flower of Egypt sought to float,
With silvered wing and amethystine throat.

While the hot sun blazed in his tower of blue
A cooling wind crept from the land of snows,
And the warm south with tender tears of dew
Drenched its white leaves when Hesperos uprose
Amid those sea-green meadows of the sky
On which the scarlet bars of sunset lie.

But when o'er wastes of lily-haunted field
The tired birds had stayed their amorous tune,
And broad and glittering like an argent shield
High in the sapphire heavens hung the moon,
Did no strange dream or evil memory make
Each tremulous petal of its blossoms shake?

Ah no! to this bright flower a thousand years
Seemed but the lingering of a summer's day,
It never knew the tide of cankering fears
Which turn a boy's gold hair to withered gray,
The dread desire of death it never knew,
Or how all folk that they were born must rue.

而夜鶯對它熾熱的愛，教牠
忘卻瑟雷斯山丘的殘酷國王，
蒼白鴿子不願再度展翅飛翔
穿越潮濕森林，春暖花開之際，
這朵埃及花兒還盼望著飄零，
撐起銀白色羽翼及紫晶的喉頸。

炎熱烈陽燒灼著藍色高塔
沁心涼風自雪地潛行，
溫暖南方柔情的露水淚珠
沾濕了它的白色葉片，
猩紅日落天空的碧綠草地
黃昏之星亦冉冉升起。

百合出沒的大地荒野
倦鳥留守牠們愛的曲調，
寬闊閃爍猶如銀白盾牌
在藍寶石天際高掛月亮，
詭譎夢境或驚悚回憶
莫不讓花瓣片片顫抖？

啊，不！這明豔之花的千年
彷彿僅僅流連一日仲夏，
它不識腐敗的恐懼狂潮
讓男孩的金髮褪色灰白，
它從不知死亡的恐懼欲望，
亦不曉出生的人必感懊悔。

For we to death with pipe and dancing go,
Nor would we pass the ivory gate again,
As some sad river wearied of its flow
Through the dull plains, the haunts of common men,
Leaps lover-like into the terrible sea!
And counts it gain to die so gloriously.

We mar our lordly strength in barren strife
With the world's legions led by clamorous care,
It never feels decay but gathers life
From the pure sunlight and the supreme air,
We live beneath Time's wasting sovereignty,
It is the child of all eternity.

我們隨笛聲與歌舞邁向死亡，
將永不再穿越象牙白色大門，
惆悵河水倦怠著、漂流著
流過蕭瑟平原、庶民住所，
如戀人縱身一躍惶惶海洋！
死得光榮輝煌。

我們平白紛爭汙損君王威權，
嘈雜喧鬧地率領世界的部隊，
永不察腐朽，而是從純真日光
和至高大氣裡，凝聚著生命，
我們活在時光衰退的統治下，
時間就是永恆的孩子。

1　希臘文為「永生」之意。

– Phèdre: To Sarah Bernhardt –

How vain and dull this common world must seem
To such a One as thou, who should'st have talked
At Florence with Mirandola, or walked
Through the cool olives of the Academe:
Thou should'st have gathered reeds from a green stream
For Goat-foot Pan's shrill piping, and have played
With the white girls in that Phaacian glade
Where grave Odysseus wakened from his dream.

Ah! surely once some urn of Attic clay
Held thy wan dust, and thou hast come again
Back to this common world so dull and vain,
For thou wert weary of the sunless day,
The heavy fields of scentless asphodel,
The loveless lips with which men kiss in Hell.

– 菲德拉¹：獻給莎拉・伯恩哈特² –

在你眼底
平凡人間必空虛徒勞，
你在翡冷翠和米蘭多拉³觸膝長談，
抑或漫步穿過學院的清涼橄欖樹：
你或許曾在翠綠清溪邊摘過蘆葦，
長著山羊足的潘神在菲阿科斯林地
與肌膚皓白的少女吹奏出尖刺笛聲，
不苟言笑的奧德修斯，美夢驚醒。

啊！阿蒂卡⁴土甕確實曾經
裝著你蠟白骨灰，而你歸返
這個空虛徒勞的平凡人間，
只因受夠舉目無日的歲月，
長滿無味長春花的沉重平原，
地獄裡，男人的唇不帶愛意地親吻。

1　《菲德拉》故事講述雅典王提修斯的妻子菲德拉，因丈夫外出戰爭未歸，以為國王已死，
　　轉而追求提修斯的兒子喜波利特斯，卻不幸遭拒。菲德拉氣憤之下向雅典王告狀自己
　　遭到非禮，國王聽信一面之詞，遂殺了兒子喜波利特斯，菲德拉得知後羞愧自盡。
2　法國的戲劇女神，菲德拉是她演繹最成功的角色之一。一八七九年，王爾德題詞，將
　　此詩獻給莎拉。
3　十五世紀義大利文藝復興時期的哲學家。
4　希臘雅典的別稱。

– Queen Henrietta Maria –

In the lone tent, waiting for victory,
She stands with eyes marred by the mists of pain,
Like some wan lily overdrenched with rain:
The clamorous clang of arms, the ensanguined sky,
War's ruin, and the wreck of chivalry,
To her proud soul no common fear can bring:
Bravely she tarrieth for her Lord the King,
Her soul a-flame with passionate ecstasy.
O Hair of Gold! O Crimson Lips! O Face
Made for the luring and the love of man!
With thee I do forget the toil and stress,
The loveless road that knows no resting place,
Time's straitened pulse, the soul's dread weariness,
My freedom and my life republican!

– 海麗塔瑪麗亞皇后 [1] –

孤零零的帳篷，等候勝利，
她杵著，任疼痛的霧氣玷汙雙眼，
猶如雨水浸濕的蒼白百合：
兵戎洪亮，血染天空，
戰爭廢墟，騎士殞落，
她驕傲的靈魂感受不到平凡惶恐：
她勇敢守候夫君國王，
靈魂熱情地狂喜燒灼。
噢，金黃的髮！噢，紅潤的唇！
噢，天生引誘男人深陷的面龐！
有了你，我忘卻磨難緊繃，
尋不著安息處的無愛路途，
光陰窘迫的搏動，惶懼靈魂的困頓，
我的自由，我的共和人生！

1　王爾德將此詩獻給英國知名女演員艾倫‧泰瑞，她在《查理一世》裡精湛詮釋海麗塔瑪麗亞皇后。

– Louis Napoleon –

Eagle of Austerlitz! where were thy wings
When far away upon a barbarous strand,
In fight unequal, by an obscure hand,
Fell the last scion of thy brood of Kings!

Poor boy! thou wilt not flaunt thy cloak of red,
Nor ride in state through Paris in the van
Of thy returning legions, but instead
Thy mother France, free and republican,

Shall on thy dead and crownless forehead place
The better laurels of a soldier's crown,
That not dishonoured should thy soul go down
To tell the mighty Sire of thy race

That France hath kissed the mouth of Liberty,
And found it sweeter than his honied bees,
And that the giant wave Democracy
Breaks on the shores where Kings lay crouched at ease.

– 拿破崙四世[1] –

奧斯特里茲之鷹！你的羽翼在哪裡？
野蠻殘暴的遙遙地平線，
天差地別的戰役，一隻不知名的手
摘下你代代國王殘存的後裔！

可憐的男孩！你不會炫耀一身紅袍，
亦無法隨軍隊凱旋歸返，
駕著榮耀篷車穿越巴黎，
你的母親法國，已是自由共和體。

殉職和無冠的平凡額髮上
理應戴上士兵的勝利榮冠，
你的靈魂不該恥於
向人民的偉大後嗣訴說

法國親吻了自由的唇，
驚覺它比蜜蜂更甘甜，
浩瀚澎湃的民主浪花
拍打國王們卑躬屈膝的海岸。

1　拿破崙三世之子，普法戰爭爆發時，戰爭失利，他與母親從法國逃至英格蘭，被視為
　　拿破崙家族的唯一希望。

– Apologia –

Is it thy will that I should wax and wane,
Barter my cloth of gold for hodden grey,
And at thy pleasure weave that web of pain
Whose brightest threads are each a wasted day?

Is it thy will—Love that I love so well—
That my Soul's House should be a tortured spot
Wherein, like evil paramours, must dwell
The quenchless flame, the worm that dieth not?

Nay, if it be thy will I shall endure,
And sell ambition at the common mart,
And let dull failure be my vestiture,
And sorrow dig its grave within my heart.

Perchance it may be better so—at least
I have not made my heart a heart of stone,
Nor starved my boyhood of its goodly feast,
Nor walked where Beauty is a thing unknown.

Many a man hath done so; sought to fence
In straitened bonds the soul that should be free,
Trodden the dusty road of common sense,
While all the forest sang of liberty,

Not marking how the spotted hawk in flight
Passed on wide pinion through the lofty air,

– 辯護 –

我的陰晴圓缺，是你的旨意，
將我的金縷衣換成蒼灰陋衣，
編織斷腸的網，是你的歡喜，
亮麗的絲線是一個個荒廢日子？

我透徹入骨的愛，是你的旨意，
我的靈魂之屋是刑房
正如邪惡情婦的閨房，住著
熄滅不了的焰火，生著永恆不死的蠕蟲？

不，我接受你的旨意，
在平民市集拍賣野心，
潰敗成了我穿戴的衣，
淒苦在我的心底掘墳。

也許這樣也好——至少
我沒讓心靈淪為化石，
不曾剝奪童年的盛宴，
未到人不識美麗之地。

人人皆是；在窘迫束縛中
尋找防衛，靈魂應當自由，
踏上塵土飛揚的常識之路，
聽整座森林高聲歡唱自由，

不留意斑點身軀的隼飛翔，
寬廣前翼，遨遊天空，

To where the steep untrodden mountain height
Caught the last tresses of the Sun God's hair.

Or how the little flower he trod upon,
The daisy, that white-feathered shield of gold,
Followed with wistful eyes the wandering sun
Content if once its leaves were aureoled.

But surely it is something to have been
The best belovèd for a little while,
To have walked hand in hand with Love, and seen
His purple wings flit once across thy smile.

Ay! though the gorgèd asp of passion feed
On my boy's heart, yet have I burst the bars,
Stood face to face with Beauty, known indeed
The Love which moves the Sun and all the stars!

飛到無人踏過的矗立山峰
捕捉太陽神最終幾絡鬈髮。

亦不留意他踩踏過的小花，
雛菊白色羽毛的金黃盾牌，
單相思雙眼緊追流浪太陽，
它的光暈籠罩葉片亦滿足。

但能夠短暫成為摯愛
自是再好不過的美事，
能執起所愛之手前進，見到
他殷紫羽翼，掠過你的笑。

是！儘管名為激情的貪婪毒蛇吞下
我的少年之心，我仍衝出圍欄，
面對美麗杵立，親眼見識
能夠移動日月星辰的愛！

– Ave Imperatrix –

Set in this stormy Northern sea,
Queen of these restless fields of tide,
England! what shall men say of thee,
Before whose feet the worlds divide?

The earth, a brittle globe of glass,
Lies in the hollow of thy hand,
And through its heart of crystal pass,
Like shadows through a twilight land,

The spears of crimson-suited war,
The long white-crested waves of fight,
And all the deadly fires which are
The torches of the lords of Night.

The yellow leopards, strained and lean,
The treacherous Russian knows so well,
With gaping blackened jaws are seen
Leap through the hail of screaming shell.

The strong sea-lion of England's wars
Hath left his sapphire cave of sea,
To battle with the storm that mars
The star of England's chivalry.

The brazen-throated clarion blows
Across the Pathan's reedy fen,

− 為女皇歡呼 −

暴風交加的奔流北海，
淘淘不絕的潮汐女王，
英格蘭！世界在你腳邊分離前，
人們將會如何形容你？

脆弱玻璃球，地球啊，
就躺在你空蕩手掌中，
水晶般的心閃逝而去，
猶如暮光之地的掠影，

一身血紅殺戮的戰矛，
白長冠毛的戰役高浪，
黑夜國王的火炬
就是那致命烈火。

黃色美洲豹，焦慮而精瘦，
狡詐莫測的俄羅斯人最懂，
可見他們墨黑色下顎大開
躍過貝殼驚叫絕響的歡呼。

英格蘭戰爭的強壯海獅
已離開他翡翠大海洞穴，
與摧毀英格蘭騎士之星
那場暴風雨搏鬥。

歌喉刺耳的喇叭聲聲吹響
穿徹了帕坦人[1]的蘆葦沼澤，

And the high steeps of Indian snows
Shake to the tread of armèd men.

And many an Afghan chief, who lies
Beneath his cool pomegranate-trees,
Clutches his sword in fierce surmise
When on the mountain-side he sees

The fleet-foot Marri scout, who comes
To tell how he hath heard afar
The measured roll of English drums
Beat at the gates of Kandahar.

For southern wind and east wind meet
Where, girt and crowned by sword and fire,
England with bare and bloody feet
Climbs the steep road of wide empire.

O lonely Himalayan height,
Grey pillar of the Indian sky,
Where saw'st thou last in clanging fight
Our wingèd dogs of Victory?

The almond groves of Samarcand,
Bokhara, where red lilies blow,
And Oxus, by whose yellow sand
The grave white-turbaned merchants go:

And on from thence to Ispahan,
The gilded garden of the sun,

全副武裝的軍隊步履堅定
震顫印度瑞雪的懸崖峭壁。

有多少阿富汗將領
躺在沁涼石榴樹下，
狂亂臆測的手，緊握著劍，
他在山坡瞥見

腳步輕快的馬里偵察兵
前來通報他的所見所聞，
英格蘭戰鼓整齊劃一
隆隆拍擊著坎達哈 [2] 城門。

南風和東風交會於
腰間佩劍、頭戴兵火的英格蘭，
赤裸流血的雙足
攀爬著浩瀚帝國的陡峭道路。

噢，寂寥孤獨的喜馬拉雅高峰，
印度穹蒼的石灰柱，
你上回何時在風火雷電的戰役
看見我們長著翅膀的勝利之犬？

撒馬爾罕 [3] 的杏木樹叢，
布哈拉 [4] 的紅百合隨風飄揚，
奧克蘇斯的黃沙岸邊
纏繞白頭巾的嚴肅商人說：

從那裡前往伊斯法罕 [5]，
太陽的鍍金花園，

Whence the long dusty caravan
Brings cedar and vermilion;

And that dread city of Cabool
Set at the mountain's scarpèd feet,
Whose marble tanks are ever full
With water for the noonday heat:

Where through the narrow straight Bazaar
A little maid Circassian
Is led, a present from the Czar
Unto some old and bearded khan,—

Here have our wild war-eagles flown,
And flapped wide wings in fiery fight;
But the sad dove, that sits alone
In England—she hath no delight.

In vain the laughing girl will lean
To greet her love with love-lit eyes:
Down in some treacherous black ravine,
Clutching his flag, the dead boy lies.

And many a moon and sun will see
The lingering wistful children wait
To climb upon their father's knee;
And in each house made desolate

Pale women who have lost their lord
Will kiss the relics of the slain—

風塵僕僕的迤邐商隊
帶來雪松和硃砂；

恐怖之城喀布爾[6]
位在護城河陡坡山腳，
大理石貯水池永遠裝滿
解除正午熱暑的水：

通過狹長羊腸般市場
一名切爾克西亞[7]姑娘
領進，是來自沙皇的贈禮
獻給垂老蓄鬚的可汗，——

我們的狂野戰鷹展翅翱翔，
烽火綿延的戰役裡拍振寬翅；
但悲傷的鴿，獨自而坐，
就在英格蘭——開心不了。

女子笑盈盈，徒勞獻殷勤，
眼神盛滿愛意，問候愛人：
詭譎多端的漆黑溝壑之下，
亡命男孩靜躺，緊握旗幟。

日日月月，將會見證
那流連徘徊的孩子思戀
空等著攀上父親的雙膝；
在每間孤寂淒涼的屋裡

失去丈夫的慘白婦女
亦將親吻死者的遺物——

Some tarnished epaulette—some sword—
Poor toys to soothe such anguished pain.

For not in quiet English fields
Are these, our brothers, lain to rest,
Where we might deck their broken shields
With all the flowers the dead love best.

For some are by the Delhi walls,
And many in the Afghan land,
And many where the Ganges falls
Through seven mouths of shifting sand.

And some in Russian waters lie,
And others in the seas which are
The portals to the East, or by
The wind-swept heights of Trafalgar.

O wandering graves! O restless sleep!
O silence of the sunless day!
O still ravine! O stormy deep!
Give up your prey! Give up your prey!

And thou whose wounds are never healed,
Whose weary race is never won,
O Cromwell's England! must thou yield
For every inch of ground a son?

Go! crown with thorns thy gold-crowned head,
Change thy glad song to song of pain;

有些肩章黯淡──有些劍身濁汙──
都是安撫心碎痛苦的可憐玩具。

我們的兄弟並非安息
在靜謐英格蘭田野裡，
在那兒疊高破裂盾牌
獻上死者鍾愛的花朵。

有些人倒在德里高牆腳，
許多人躺在阿富汗國土，
更多人在恆河墜入飄蕩
七個河口黃沙滾滾奔流。

有些人倒臥在俄羅斯水域，
其他人則漂浮通往
那東方大門的海洋，抑或
勁風吹拂的特拉法加高峰。

噢，流浪的墳墓！噢，不得安寧之眠！
噢，終不見日的沉默！
噢，幽靜的深谷！噢，暴風襲擊深處！
放你的獵物走！放你的獵物走！

而你，傷口永遠無法痊癒，
永遠贏不了這場倦怠賽跑，
噢，克倫威爾的英格蘭！你必須
為每寸土，放棄一個孩子？

去吧！金黃頭頂加冕荊棘，
愉快旋律演變成傷痛之歌；

Wind and wild wave have got thy dead,
And will not yield them back again.

Wave and wild wind and foreign shore
Possess the flower of English land—
Lips that thy lips shall kiss no more,
Hands that shall never clasp thy hand.

What profit now that we have bound
The whole round world with nets of gold,
If hidden in our heart is found
The care that groweth never old?

What profit that our galleys ride,
Pine-forest-like, on every main?
Ruin and wreck are at our side,
Grim warders of the House of pain.

Where are the brave, the strong, the fleet?
Where is our English chivalry?
Wild grasses are their burial-sheet,
And sobbing waves their threnody.

O loved ones lying far away,
What word of love can dead lips send!
O wasted dust! O senseless clay!
Is this the end! is this the end!

Peace, peace! we wrong the noble dead
To vex their solemn slumber so;

強風狂浪已吞噬你的死者，
再也不會將他們一一歸還。

狂風巨浪以及陌生海岸
占有了英格蘭國度的花——
你的唇再親吻不了的唇，
永遠不會緊握你手的手。

我們拿黃金網纏繞世界
如今可有獲得什麼好處？
倘若深藏在我心
哀愁永遠不消退。

我們的戰艦出航，彷若松林，
大海聳立，帶來了什麼好處？
廢墟和船難歷歷在目，
傷痛殿堂的無情獄吏。

英勇強壯敏捷的人上哪去？
英格蘭的騎士精神上哪去？
野草就是他們的裹屍布，
啜泣海浪則是他們的輓歌。

噢，躺臥於遙遠他鄉的摯愛，
死亡之唇豈能傳遞愛的絮語！
噢，荒蕪的飛塵！噢，無知的泥土！
難道這就是終點！難道這就是終點！

安息吧，安息！我們怠慢高貴亡者，
打擾了他們的神聖睡眠；

Though childless, and with thorn-crowned head,
Up the steep road must England go,

Yet when this fiery web is spun,
Her watchmen shall descry from far
The young Republic like a sun
Rise from these crimson seas of war.

儘管無子無嗣，頭卻戴著荊棘皇冠，
英格蘭必步上陡峭道路，

當熱烈激情的絲網編織，
她的看守人將認出遠方
那初生的共和國，彷彿旭日
自猩紅戰海冉冉升起。

1　印度西北邊境的阿富汗人。

2　阿富汗歷任帝國的首都。

3　中亞地區的歷史名城，現為烏茲別克的舊都兼第二大城。

4　烏茲別克西南方的城鎮。

5　伊朗第三大城。

6　阿富汗首都，亦是最大城。

7　歐俄的高加索民族。

〈希律王的目光 The Eyes of Herod〉
希律王愛上繼女莎樂美。莎樂美藉此向希律王求取施洗者約翰的頭顱。

〈七重紗舞 The Stomach Dance〉
王爾德曾說比亞茲萊是「唯一知道七重紗舞為何、也是唯一能看見這不可見之舞的藝術家。」

– Pan: Double Villanelle –

I.
O goat-foot God of Arcady!
This modern world is grey and old,
And what remains to us of thee?

No more the shepherd lads in glee
Throw apples at thy wattled fold,
O goat-foot God of Arcady!

Nor through the laurels can one see
Thy soft brown limbs, thy beard of gold
And what remains to us of thee?

And dull and dead our Thames would be,
For here the winds are chill and cold,
O goat-loot God of Arcady!

Then keep the tomb of Helice,
Thine olive-woods, thy vine-clad wold,
And what remains to us of thee?

Though many an unsung elegy
Sleeps in the reeds our rivers hold,
O goat-foot God of Arcady!
Ah, what remains to us of thee?

- 潘神：二重田園歌 -

I.
噢，長著山羊足的阿卡迪神！
現代世界昏暗陳舊，
你留下什麼給我們？

牧羊童已經無法再歡天喜地，
蘋果朝開滿金合歡的原野扔，
噢，長著山羊足的阿卡迪神！

無人能從桂冠看出
你柔軟的褐色四肢，你的金黃鬍鬚，
你留下什麼給我們？

我們的泰晤士河水死氣沉沉，
這裡的冷風颼颼蕭瑟，
噢，長著山羊足的阿卡迪神！

保留海利斯城的墳，
橄欖樹林，葡萄樹遍野，
你留下什麼給我們？

雖尚未唱吟的無盡輓歌
在我們河裡的蘆葦沉睡，
噢，長著山羊足的阿卡迪神！
啊，你留下什麼給我們？

II.
Ah, leave the hills of Arcady,
Thy satyrs and their wanton play,
This modern world hath need of thee.

No nymph or Faun indeed have we,
For Faun and nymph are old and grey,
Ah, leave the hills of Arcady!

This is the land where liberty
Lit grave-browed Milton on his way,
This modern world hath need of thee!

A land of ancient chivalry
Where gentle Sidney saw the day,
Ah, leave the hills of Arcady!

This fierce sea-lion of the sea,
This England lacks some stronger lay,
This modern world hath need of thee!

Then blow some trumpet loud and free,
And give thine oaten pipe away,
Ah, leave the hills of Arcady!
This modern world hath need of thee!

II.
啊，離開阿卡迪山丘吧，
帶著撒泰兒[1]和他們的縱情，
現代世界需要你。

我們著實沒有仙女或牧神，
牧神仙女垂垂老矣，灰髮蒼蒼，
啊，離開阿卡迪山丘吧！

這是塊自由國土，
點燃眉頭深鎖的米爾頓靈感，
現代世界需要你！

充滿古老騎士精神的國度，
溫儒的錫德尼[2]預知著這天，
啊，離開阿卡迪山丘吧！

這隻來自大海的勇猛海獅，
英格蘭缺乏更熱烈的歡愉，
現代世界需要你！

快吹響自由的號角，
交出你的燕麥稈笛，
啊，離開阿卡迪山丘吧！
現代世界需要你！

1　希臘神話裡，半人半羊的牧神，縱情飲酒狂歡。
2　Sir Philip Sidney（1554-1586），十六世紀的英國詩人兼政治家。

– Sen Artysty; or, The Artist's Dream –

I too have had my dreams: ay, known indeed
The crowded visions of a fiery youth
Which haunt me still.

Methought that once I lay,
Within some garden-close, what time the Spring
Breaks like a bird from Winter, and the sky
Is sapphire-vaulted. The pure air was soft,
And the deep grass I lay on soft as air.
The strange and secret life of the young trees
Swelled in the green and tender bark, or burst
To buds of sheathèd emerald; violets
Peered from their nooks of hiding, half afraid
Of their own loveliness; the vermeil rose
Opened its heart, and the bright star-flower
Shone like a star of morning. Butterflies,
In painted liveries of brown and gold,
Took the shy bluebells as their pavilions
And seats of pleasaunce; overhead a bird
Made snow of all the blossoms as it flew
To charm the woods with singing: the whole world
Seemed waking to delight!
And yet—and yet—.
My soul was filled with leaden heaviness:
I had no joy in Nature; what to me,
Ambition's slave, was crimson-stainèd rose,
Or the gold-sceptred crocus? The bright bird

– 藝術家之夢 –

我懷抱許多夢想：你我皆知，
烈火青春的種種遠景
至今依舊，縈繞不去。

我想，我要是躺下，
倒在某座鄰近花園，春季便如
飛離寒冬的鳥兒，天空
無比青翠。純淨空氣輕柔，
我躺臥輕如空氣的青青草地。
那奇異而奧祕的幼樹生命，
綠意盎然的稚嫩樹皮膨脹，抑或
綠茵包裹的花苞綻放；紫羅蘭
從躲藏的角落窺視，半是
為了自己的美貌害怕；朱紅薔薇
盛開它一顆心，明豔琉璃苣
猶如晨星閃耀。蝴蝶，
身著塗抹棕金色調的彩衣，
占據涼亭裡的羞怯風信子，
當作他們愉悅的椅子；頭頂飛過的鳥兒
驚得花朵盛開雪白，
用歌喉對森林施魔法：全世界
似乎歡欣覺醒！
可是啊──可是──。
我的靈魂沉重猶如鉛塊：
大自然無法帶給我歡樂；對於我，
這野心的奴隸，豔紅色澤的薔薇，
抑或金黃權杖般的番紅花為何物？明快鳥兒的

Sang out of tune for me, and the sweet flowers
Seemed but a pageant, and an unreal show
That mocked my heart; for, like the fabled snake
That stings itself to anguish, so I lay,
Self-tortured, self-tormented.
The day crept
Unheeded on the dial, till the sun
Dropt, purple-sailed, into the gorgeous East,
When, from the fiery heart of that great orb,
Came One whose shape of beauty far outshone
The most bright vision of this common earth.
Girt was she in a robe more white than flame,
Or furnace-heated brass; upon her head
She bare a laurel crown, and like a star
That falls from the high heaven suddenly,
Passed to my side.
Then kneeling low, I cried,
'O much-desired! O long-waited for!
Immortal Glory! Great world-conqueror!
O let me not die crownless; once, at least,
Let thine imperial laurels bind my brows,
Ignoble else. Once let the clarion-note
And trump of loud ambition sound my name,
And for the rest I care not.'
Then to me,
In gentle voice, the angel made reply:
'Child ignorant of the true happiness,
Nor knowing life's best wisdom, thou wert made
For light, and love, and laughter; not to waste
Thy youth in shooting arrows at the sun,

歌曲走調，甜美花兒
似乎只是炫耀，猶如不切實際的表演
嘲弄我的心；於是，猶如寓言裡的蛇
刺痛自己內心哀愁，我亦躺著，
自我折磨，自我鞭笞。
白晝漫不經心地
徐徐爬行日晷，直到日落
披上嫣紫，航向燦爛東方，
從那顆碩大圓球的火熱之心，
誕生超越凡塵俗世的美豔輪廓
美過最光耀鮮明的景象。
她穿了一襲衣袍，白過火焰，
或熔爐燒製的黃銅；她的頭頂
戴了只月桂冠，彷若巍峨天庭
瞬間殞落的孤星，
降落我身側。
於是我壓低身子，呼喊，
「噢，我千呼萬喚的你！噢，我望穿秋水的你！
不朽榮耀！偉大的世界征服者！
噢，別讓我頭無桂冠地離開人世；至少，
用你尊貴月桂葉妝點我的眉，
否則我卑微低賤。用響亮野心的
小號曲調及喇叭，吹響我的名號，
其他我無欲無求。」
對著我，
天使用溫柔嗓音，回答：
「不識真實幸福，
不懂人生崇高智慧的孩子，你的生命
是為了光，為了愛，為了笑而生；不是為了
虛擲青春朝太陽射箭，

Or nurturing that ambition in thy soul
Whose deadly poison will infect thy heart,
Marring all joy and gladness! Tarry here,
In the sweet confines of this garden-close,
Whose level meads and glades delectable
Invite for pleasure; the wild bird that wakes
These silent dells with sudden melody
Shall be thy playmate; and each flower that blows
Shall twine itself unbidden in thy hair—
Garland more meet for thee than the dread weight
Of Glory's laurel-wreath.'
　'Ah! fruitless gifts,'
I cried, unheeding of her prudent word,
　'Are all such mortal flowers, whose brief lives
Are bounded by the dawn and setting sun.
The anger of the noon can wound the rose,
And the rain rob the crocus of its gold;
But thine immortal coronal of Fame,
Thy crown of deathless laurel, this alone
Age cannot harm, nor winter's icy tooth
Pierce to its hurt, nor common things profane.'
No answer made the angel, but her face
Dimmed with the mists of pity.
Then methought
That from mine eyes, wherein ambition's torch
Burned with its latest and most ardent flame,
Flashed forth two level beams of straightened light,
Beneath whose fulgent fires the laurel crown
Twisted and curled, as when the Sirian star
Withers the ripening corn, and one pale leaf

也不是為了在靈魂餵養野心而生，
野心的致命毒液會腐蝕你的心，
將所有喜悅與歡樂破壞殆盡！待在這兒，
就在這鄰近花園的甜蜜空間，
一望無際的草地和甘美林地
迎接歡愉；野鳥的音符旋律
突如其來地驚醒幽靜小谷地，
牠該是你的玩伴；而朵朵搖曳生姿的花
都應該主動盤繞在你的秀髮上——
這是遠比榮耀桂冠的驚人重量
更加適合你的花環。」
「啊！徒勞無果的禮物，」
我驚嘆，不顧她深謀遠慮的話語，
「這些凡世俗花，短暫生命
終將受到晨曦落日所累。
正午的震怒可以燙傷薔薇，
磅礡雨水亦可奪走番紅花的金黃；
但是名譽的不朽皇冠，
唯獨不死的月桂榮冠，
年年歲歲終無法摧殘，寒冬的冰凍尖牙
無法穿刺破壞，俗事亦不可褻瀆。」
天使未搭腔，遺憾的迷霧
遮蔽陰暗了她的臉龐。
然後，就我所知，
我的雙眼，重新燃起
野心的火炬，
熊熊火焰噴射出兩道筆直光束，
光輝耀眼的火光底下
月桂冠捲曲歪扭，猶如天狼星
枯萎成熟穀粒，一片蒼白葉子

Fell on my brow; and I leapt up and felt
The mighty pulse of Fame, and heard far off
The sound of many nations praising me!

One fiery-coloured moment of great life!
And then—how barren was the nations' praise!
How vain the trump of Glory! Bitter thorns
Were in that laurel leaf, whose toothèd barbs
Burned and bit deep till fire and red flame
Seemed to feed full upon my brain, and make
The garden a bare desert.
With wild hands
I strove to tear it from my bleeding brow,
But all in vain; and with a dolorous cry
That paled the lingering stars before their time,
I waked at last, and saw the timorous dawn
Peer with grey face into my darkened room,
And would have deemed it a mere idle dream
But for this restless pain that gnaws my heart,
And the red wounds of thorns upon my brow.

凋落至我的眉梢；我驚嚇一跳，
感受到名譽的強大脈動，聽聞遠處
傳來無數國度讚譽我的聲音！

美好人生神采飛揚的一刻！
然而——各國讚揚竟如此貧瘠！
榮耀的號角多麼空虛！苦澀荊棘
就藏在月桂葉裡，它的利齒
芒刺燒灼，深深啃咬，直到烈火和紅色火焰
彷彿完全腐蝕我的大腦，將花園
化作一片寂寥荒漠。
我狂亂揮舞著雙手，
試圖從淌血眉宇間，奮力摘下它，
卻徒勞無功；我發出了沉痛哀號，
讓流連忘返的星斗提前微弱黯淡，
我終甦醒，望見提心吊膽的黎明，
灰白臉龐眺探著我的漆黑房間，
內心暗忖這只是場空白無趣的夢，
但啃噬著我心的悲痛無止無盡，
眉宇上，荊棘留下一道血紅傷口。

– Libertatis Sacra Fames –

Albeit nurtured in democracy,
And liking best that state republican
Where every man is Kinglike and no man
Is crowned above his fellows, yet I see,
Spite of this modern fret for Liberty,
Better the rule of One, whom all obey,
Than to let clamorous demagogues betray
Our freedom with the kiss of anarchy.
Wherefore I love them not whose hands profane
Plant the red flag upon the piled-up street
For no right cause, beneath whose ignorant reign
Arts, Culture, Reverence, Honour, all things fade,
Save Treason and the dagger of her trade,
And Murder with his silent bloody feet.

– 自由的聖潔飢荒 –

儘管接受民主餵養，
最愛的還是共和國
人人皆為君王，
無人加冕高於同胞。
雖現代苦苦追求自由，
一君獨統，眾聲應允，
都好過喧嘩嘈雜的煽動叛徒，
無政府之吻背叛我們的自由。
因此我熱愛的不是褻瀆的雙手，
鮮紅旗幟插上路障高堆的街頭，
倘若非出於正義，無知統治下
藝術，文化，景仰，榮譽，萬物皆消逝，
僅存背叛與她的匕首，
以及謀殺與他沉默沾血的雙腳。

– Sonnet to Liberty –

Not that I love thy children, whose dull eyes
See nothing save their own unlovely woe,
Whose minds know nothing, nothing care to know,—
But that the roar of thy Democracies,
Thy reigns of Terror, thy great Anarchies,
Mirror my wildest passions like the sea,—
And give my rage a brother—! Liberty!
For this sake only do thy dissonant cries
Delight my discreet soul, else might all kings
By bloody knout or treacherous cannonades
Rob nations of their rights inviolate
And I remain unmoved—and yet, and yet,
These Christs that die upon the barricades,
God knows it I am with them, in some things.

– 自由之詩 –

我並不愛你的孩子，他們的呆滯雙眼
只看見不討喜的自憐哀傷，視若無睹，
他們腦袋空無一物，亦不願深入理解，——
但，你民主的咆哮，
你恐懼的執政，你偉大的無政府狀態，
猶如一面鏡海，映照出我的狂野熱情，——
為我的憤怒帶來一名手足——！自由！
唯獨如此，你不和諧的悲鳴
為我那謹慎的靈魂帶來喜悅，否則所有國王
皆可血腥鞭笞，或狡詐砲擊，
奪走了國家不可侵犯的權利
而我無動於衷——然而啊然而，
這些死於路障擋牆的基督們，
上帝知曉某些信念上，我與他們同在。

– Tædium Vitæ[1] –

To stab my youth with desparate knives, to wear
This paltrey age's gaudy livery,
To let each base hand filch my treasury,
To mesh my soul within a woman's hair,
And be mere Fortune's lackeyed groom,—I swear
I love it not! These things are less to me
Than the thin foam that frets upon the sea,
Less than the thistle-down of summer air
Which hath no seed: better to stand aloof
Far from these slanderous fools who mock my life
Knowing me not, better the lowliest roof
Fit for the meanest hind to sojourn in,
Than to go back to that hoarse cave of strife
Where my white soul first kissed the mouth of sin.

－ 厭世 －

絕望的刀刺進了我的青春，
穿戴空白世代的俗豔裝束，
讓一隻隻手竊取我的財富，
將我的靈魂編入女人的髮，
當命運使喚的新郎，——我發誓
我並不願！這一切對我而言
都不及啃噬海洋的細微泡沫，
不及夏季空氣裡沒有種子的
薊花冠毛：最好冷漠遠離
惡意毀謗我、嘲諷我人生的愚者，
他們不識我；最好留居
低等下人的簡陋屋頂，
而不是歸返紛爭的粗啞洞窟，
在那兒，我潔白的靈魂初次親吻罪的唇。

1　標題為拉丁文。

– Camma –

As one who poring on a Grecian urn
Scans the fair shapes some Attic hand hath made,
God with slim goddess, goodly man with maid,
And for their beauty's sake is loth to turn
And face the obvious day, must I not yearn
For many a secret moon of indolent bliss,
When in the midmost shrine of Artemis
I see thee standing, antique-limbed, and stern?

And yet—methinks I'd rather see thee play
That serpent of old Nile, whose witchery
Made Emperors drunken,—come, great Egypt, shake
Our stage with all thy mimic pageants! Nay,
I am grown sick of unreal passions, make
The world thine Actium, me thine Antony!

– 加瑪 [1] –

當他凝視著希臘古甕，
掃視阿蒂卡之手塑造的美麗形體，
纖細女神旁的男神，少女與美男，
憎恨也因為他們的美貌轉身
面對必然的那天，我難道
在阿緹密斯神殿之心，
看見你杵著，古老軀體，堅定不搖，
不得渴望那安逸幸福的神祕月亮？

但我——寧可看你扮演
古老尼羅河的蛇，牠的妖術
教皇帝傾心，——來，偉大埃及，
以你虛假的歷史劇，震撼舞台！不，
不真實的熱情令我厭惡，就讓世界
成為你的雅克興 [2]，我當你的安東尼 [3]！

---

1 羅馬時代的希臘作家普魯塔克故事裡的加拉太公主，亦是狩獵女神阿緹密斯的女祭司。
   王爾德將本詩獻給一八八一年演出加瑪的艾倫．泰瑞，期待看見她扮演埃及豔后克麗
   奧佩脫拉。
2 位於希臘西方外海，埃及豔后參與羅馬帝國內戰，在雅克興戰役敗北時自盡，結束
   埃及三千多年歷史。
3 克麗奧佩脫拉的情人，內戰絕望之時安東尼決定自盡，最後死在埃及豔后身旁，她則
   利用毒蛇自殺。

〈莎樂美的梳妝室一 The Toilette of Salome I〉
比亞茲萊在梳妝室裡放置了許多東方物件，如花瓶、漆器等器物。

– 印象：剪影輪廓 –

灰色沙洲點綴海洋斑斑，
死氣沉沉的風唱走了調，
月亮猶如枯萎凋謝樹葉
被吹過風雨交加的海灣。

黯淡沙灘上清晰蝕刻
一艘黑船：水手男孩
喜孜孜地輕率攀上船，
面帶笑容，手閃亮著。

頭頂麻鷸傳出悲鳴，
年輕褐頸的收割人
穿過幽暗高地草皮，
彷如襯在天際線的片片剪影。

– Impressions: Les Silhouettes –

The sea is flecked with bars of grey,
The dull dead wind is out of tune,
And like a withered leaf the moon
Is blown across the stormy bay.

Etched clear upon the pallid sand
The black boat lies: a sailor boy

Clambers aboard in careless joy
With laughing face and gleaming hand.

And overhead the curlews cry,
Where through the dusky upland grass
The young brown-throated reapers pass,
Like silhouettes against the sky.

〈莎樂美的梳妝室二 The Toilette of Salome II〉

– Impressions: La Fuite de la Lune –

To outer senses there is peace,
A dreamy peace on either hand,
Deep silence in the shadowy land,
Deep silence where the shadows cease.

Save for a cry that echoes shrill
From some lone bird disconsolate;
A corncrake calling to its mate;
The answer from the misty hill.

And suddenly the moon withdraws
Her sickle from the lightening skies,
And to her sombre cavern flies,
Wrapped in a veil of yellow gauze.

– 印象：月色出走 –

表面的感受為平靜，
兩手掌握夢幻寧靜，
黑影籠罩的土地幽深恬謐，
黑影退卻後亦幽深恬謐。

除了尖銳回音劃破的哭嚎，
來自那悲不自勝的孤鳥；
長腳秧雞聲聲呼喚伴侶；
迷霧繚繞的山丘傳來回聲。

霎時從雷電交加天空，
月娘收回了她的鐮刀，
隱退回她的幽幽巢洞，
裹在淡黃薄巧面紗裡。

– Impression: Le Réveillon –

The sky is laced with fitful red,
The circling mists and shadows flee,
The dawn is rising from the sea,
Like a white lady from her bed.

And jagged brazen arrows fall
Athwart the feathers of the night,
And a long wave of yellow light
Breaks silently on tower and hall,

And spreading wide across the wold
Wakes into flight some fluttering bird,
And all the chestnut tops are stirred,
And all the branches streaked with gold.

– 印象：新年前夕 –

天空繫上斷斷續續的紅，
繚繞迷霧和陰影竄逃，
黎明自海面冉冉躍升，
恍如白皙淑女床畔起身。

黃銅箭參差不齊墜落
斜穿過黑夜裡的羽毛，
一道悠長的昏黃光波
悄然劃破高塔與廳堂，

幅員遼闊四射荒原，
慌鳥拍振羽翼飛舞，
栗樹梢頭全數驚動，
黃金遍灑根根枝椏。

– Hélas! –

To drift with every passion till my soul
Is a stringed lute on which all winds can play,
Is it for this that I have given away
Mine ancient wisdom, and austere control?
Methinks my life is a twice-written scroll
Scrawled over on some boyish holiday
With idle songs for pipe and virelay,
Which do but mar the secret of the whole.
Surely that was a time I might have trod
The sunlit heights, and from life's dissonance
Struck one clear chord to reach the ears of God:
is that time dead? lo! with a little rod
I did but touch the honey of romance—
And must I lose a soul's inheritance?

– 嗚呼！ –

隨熱情——漂浮移動，直到靈魂
成了無風不可彈奏的上弦詩琴，
我為此，付出了
我的古老智慧，與清苦嚴峻的自我掌控？
我以為人生是二次複寫的羊皮卷，
在孩子氣的假期，盡情潦草塗鴉，
寫滿笛子和雙韻短詩的無聊歌曲，
卻只汙損了全部祕密。
當時我確實曾踏遍
日光照耀的高山，從生命的不和諧
敲擊出清脆和弦，傳送上帝耳裡：
那段光陰是否已逝？你瞧！我用小小一根荊條
確實觸到了羅曼史的蜜糖——
我是否必喪失靈魂的遺產？

– The Harlot's House –

We caught the tread of dancing feet,
We loitered down the moonlit street,
And stopped beneath the harlot's house.

Inside, above the din and fray,
We heard the loud musicians play
The "Treues Liebes Herz" of Strauss.

Like strange mechanical grotesques,
Making fantastic arabesques,
The shadows raced across the blind.

We watched the ghostly dancers spin
To sound of horn and violin,
Like black leaves wheeling in the wind.

Like wire-pulled automatons,
Slim silhouetted skeletons
Went sidling through the slow quadrille,

They took each other by the hand,
And danced a stately saraband;
Their laughter echoed thin and shrill.

Sometimes a clockwork puppet pressed
A phantom lover to her breast,
Sometimes they seemed to try to sing.

– 迎春閣 –

我們捕捉到舞動雙足的踩踏，
我們在月光小徑上流連忘返，
且在迎春閣下方停止了步伐。

室內，頭頂燈光昏暗疲憊，
我們聽見了樂師嘈嘈彈奏，
是史特勞斯[1]的真愛之心。

猶如機械的奇異詭譎，
曼妙的芭蕾舞姿驚豔，
窗簾後方，黑影疾疾。

我們凝望著恍若鬼魅的舞者
隨著號角和小提琴樂音旋轉，
彷彿在風中婆娑起舞的黑葉。

猶如絲線操縱的機械人，
她們以纖瘦的輪廓骨架
滑著緩慢的方陣舞步態，

她們執手躍動，
薩拉邦德舞曲莊嚴；
尖銳纖細笑聲迴盪。

發條人偶彷若鬼情人
偶爾倚在她胸前，
偶爾又似欲歌唱。

Sometimes a horrible marionette
Came out, and smaoked its cigarette
Upon the steps like a live thing.

Then, turning to my love, I said,
"The dead are dancing with the dead,
The dust is whirling with the dust."

But she—she heard the violin,
And left my side, and entered in:
Love passed into the house of lust.

Then suddenly the tune went false,
The shadows wearied of the waltz,
The shadows ceased to wheel and whirl.

And down the long and silent street,
The dawn, with silver-sandalled feet,
Crept like a frightened girl.

可怖的牽線木偶
偶爾現形，抽著香菸
在台階上，活靈活現。

接著，我轉向愛人：
「亡者與亡者共舞，
塵埃和塵埃周旋。」

但她──她耳聞小提琴聲，
離開我身側，進入室內：
愛情亦淪為欲望之屋。

接著剎那間，曲調走音，
跳著圓舞曲的舞者疲憊，
陰影逐漸不再打轉迴旋。

沿著那漫長靜謐的街道，
黎明穿著銀色涼鞋的腳，
猶如驚懼女孩匍匐潛行。

1　Johann Strauss II（1825-1899），十九世紀奧地利作曲家，其圓舞曲最為著稱。

– The New Remorse –

The sin was mine; I did not understand.
So now is music prisoned in her cave,
Save where some ebbing desultory wave
Frets with its restless whirls this meagre strand.
And in the withered hollow of this land
Hath Summer dug herself so deep a grave,
That hardly can the leaden willow crave
One silver blossom from keen Winter's hand.

But who is this who cometh by the shore?
(Nay, love, look up and wonder!) Who is this
Who cometh in dyed garments from the South?
It is thy new-found Lord, and he shall kiss
The yet unravished roses of thy mouth,
And I shall weep and worship, as before.

– 嶄新的痛悔 –

我鑄下了罪；當初懵懂無知。
而今，樂音禁錮在她的巢穴，
除了散漫退潮的海浪無盡
迴旋拍打在那貧脊的淺灘。
在這塊土地的枯萎空洞裡
夏季為自己鑿了深深墓地，
鉛般沉重的垂柳幾乎無法
渴求寒冬手中的一朵銀花。

但來到沙岸的人究竟是誰？
（不，親愛的，仰頭讚嘆！）是誰
身著染色衣裳自南方降臨？
那人是你嶄新誕生的主人，他應親吻
你尚未狂喜的唇畔薔薇，
我則悲泣崇拜，一如過往。

– Canzonet –

I have no store
Of gryphon-guarded gold;
Now, as before,
Bare is the shepherd's fold.
Rubies nor pearls
Have I to gem thy throat;
Yet woodland girls
Have loved the shepherd's note.

Then pluck a reed
And bid me sing to thee,
For I would feed
Thine ears with melody,
Who art more fair
Than fairest fleur-de-lys,
More sweet and rare
Than sweetest ambergris.

What dost thou fear?
Young Hyacinth is slain,
Pan is not here,
And will not come again.
No horned Faun
Treads down the yellow leas,
No God at dawn
Steals through the olive trees.

– 抒情小調 –

我並未擁有
獅鷲獸守護的黃金；
而一如既往，
牧羊人的羊圈空瘠。
我沒有紅寶石或珍珠
可以妝點你的喉頸；
但森林地裡的女孩
愛過牧羊人的音符。

摘下一枝蘆葦
命我唱給你聽，
我要用旋律
餵養你的耳，
你的美更勝
那最豔麗的鳶尾，
絕世甜美更勝
甘美的龍涎香。

你在恐懼什麼？
少年雅欽多[1]已歿，
潘神也不在了，
再也不會歸來。
羊角牧神也不會
走過黃澄的草原，
黎明時分不會有神祇
偷偷摸摸穿越橄欖樹叢。

Hylas is dead,
Nor will he e'er divine
Those little red
Rose-petalled lips of thine.
On the high hill
No ivory dryads play,
Silver and still
Sinks the sad autumn day.

海拉斯已歿，
他也將無法預想
你玫瑰花瓣般的
小紅唇。
高山上
象牙白的森林精靈不再嬉戲，
哀愁寡歡的秋日
銀色靜止地沉澱。

1　希臘神話中，雅欽多死於阿波羅誤擲的鐵餅，從他血泊中長出的花，則是風信子。

– The Ballad of Reading Gaol (excerption) –

I.
He did not wear his scarlet coat,
For blood and wine are red,
And blood and wine were on his hands
When they found him with the dead,
The poor dead woman whom he loved,
  And murdered in her bed.

He walked amongst the Trial Men
In a suit of shabby grey;
A cricket cap was on his head,
And his step seemed light and gay;
But I never saw a man who looked
So wistfully at the day.

I never saw a man who looked
With such a wistful eye
Upon that little tent of blue
Which prisoners call the sky,
And at every drifting cloud that went
With sails of silver by.

I walked, with other souls in pain,
Within another ring,
And was wondering if the man had done
A great or little thing,

- 瑞丁監獄之歌 (節錄) -

I.
他並未穿戴那猩紅外衫，
因鮮血與葡萄酒已紅，
他手上滿是血與酒，
當他與死者經人發現時，
他心愛的可憐已逝女人，
在她的床上慘遭謀害。

他隨著判官邁步前進，
一身陋衣蒼灰；
頭上戴了頂鴨舌帽，
腳步彷彿愉快輕盈；
我卻從未見過一個男人
像這天那般地愁悶。

我從未見過一個男人
眼神是如此愁悶
凝望那蔚藍小帳篷
囚犯所謂的天空，
望著每朵飄移浮雲
隨著銀色船帆閃逝。

我走著，和其他痛苦靈魂，
咱們兜成了一個圈子，
我納悶這男人可犯下
滔天大罪，抑或小惡，

When a voice behind me whispered low,
"That fellow's got to swing."

Dear Christ! the very prison walls
Suddenly seemed to reel,
And the sky above my head became
Like a casque of scorching steel;
And, though I was a soul in pain,
My pain I could not feel.

I only knew what hunted thought
Quickened his step, and why
He looked upon the garish day
With such a wistful eye;
The man had killed the thing he loved
And so he had to die.

Yet each man kills the thing he loves
By each let this be heard,
Some do it with a bitter look,
Some with a flattering word,
The coward does it with a kiss,
The brave man with a sword!

Some kill their love when they are young,
And some when they are old;
Some strangle with the hands of Lust,
Some with the hands of Gold:
The kindest use a knife, because
The dead so soon grow cold.

此刻身後傳來了低語，
「那傢伙的頸部當該套索。」

我的天！整座監獄牆面
剎那間似乎天旋地轉，
頭頂的天空變得
彷若一頂灼熱的鋼盔；
而我雖亦是痛苦靈魂，
卻感受不到自身的痛。

我這才明白是怎樣的憂煩
加快他的步伐，又為何
他望向這光輝燦爛的一天
眼底竟蒙上如此愁悶；
這男人殺了他的摯愛
他必須為此償命。

但誰不扼殺自己的摯愛？
不妨聽聽每個人怎麼說，
有人是用苛刻眼神，
有人則是奉承美言，
懦夫用的是一個吻，
勇者伸出一把劍！

有人青春時殺了摯愛，
有人則等到垂垂老矣；
有人用貪欲的雙手勒斃，
有人以黃金般的手屠殺：
最善良的人揮刀，只因
逝者遺體不久就會冷冰。

〈舞者的獎賞 The Dancer's Reward〉
「誰不扼殺自己的摯愛？」

〈高潮 The Climax〉
莎樂美吻了施洗者約翰……

Some love too little, some too long,
Some sell, and others buy;
Some do the deed with many tears,
And some without a sigh:
For each man kills the thing he loves,
Yet each man does not die.

He does not die a death of shame
On a day of dark disgrace,
Nor have a noose about his neck,
Nor a cloth upon his face,
Nor drop feet foremost through the floor
Into an empty place

He does not sit with silent men
Who watch him night and day;
Who watch him when he tries to weep,
And when he tries to pray;
Who watch him lest himself should rob
The prison of its prey.

He does not wake at dawn to see
Dread figures throng his room,
The shivering Chaplain robed in white,
The Sheriff stern with gloom,
And the Governor all in shiny black,
With the yellow face of Doom.

有人愛得太深，有人愛得太淺，
有人拿錢買，有人換來錢；
有人下手時淚水潰堤，
有人不帶一聲嘆息：
每個人都殺了自己的摯愛，
每個人卻氣息尚在。

他並未羞愧死去
在這黑暗恥辱的一天，
頸部並未纏繞絞索，
臉孔亦無蓋上布塊，
雙腳未先穿過地板而落
墜入一處空蕩坑洞

他未與沉默男人並肩而坐，
他們日夜看守他；
在他準備流淚時守著他，
與他試著祈禱時；
他們守著他，深怕他會搶奪
監牢裡的獵物。

他並未在黎明甦醒，未看見
威望人物湧入他房間，
顫抖的牧師一身白袍，
司法長露出陰鬱厲色，
而獄長渾身烏黑閃耀，
帶著末日般蠟黃臉色。

He does not rise in piteous haste
To put on convict-clothes,
While some coarse-mouthed Doctor gloats, and notes
Each new and nerve-twitched pose,
Fingering a watch whose little ticks
Are like horrible hammer-blows.

He does not know that sickening thirst
That sands one's throat, before
The hangman with his gardener's gloves
Slips through the padded door,
And binds one with three leathern thongs,
That the throat may thirst no more.

He does not bend his head to hear
The Burial Office read,
Nor, while the terror of his soul
Tells him he is not dead,
Cross his own coffin, as he moves
Into the hideous shed.

He does not stare upon the air
Through a little roof of glass;
He does not pray with lips of clay
For his agony to pass;
Nor feel upon his shuddering cheek
The kiss of Caiaphas.

他並未恭敬地匆促起身
穿戴罪犯的囚服，
言談粗鄙的醫生幸災樂禍，留意
他每刻牽動神經的每個姿態，
手撥弄著錶，小指針
恍若聲聲落下的恐怖鐵鎚。

他不識那教人難忍的乾渴
堵塞喉嚨的感受，直到
戴上行刑手套的劊子手
穿越那扇沉重厚門，
對著他繫綁三圈皮繩，
他的喉嚨將不再乾渴。

他不低頭聆聽
喪葬官的念念有詞，
當靈魂的驚恐
告訴他生命尚未步入尾聲，
他亦未越過棺木，而是進入
那鄙陋的刑屋。

他並未緊瞅著天空，
目光穿越小小的玻璃屋頂；
他並未用黏土般緊閉的唇
禱告苦痛能快點逝去；
亦無在他顫慄的面頰
感受到該亞法[1]的吻。

_____

1　猶太教的大祭司，策劃並參與耶穌的謀殺。

國家圖書館出版品預行編目資料

絕望的刀刺進了我的青春：王爾德詩選 I ／王爾德著；
張家綺譯 .———初版———臺中市：好讀，2018.06
面；　公分，———（典藏經典；115）

ISBN 978-986-178-457-1（平裝）
873.51　　　　　　　　　　　　　　　107005787

好讀出版

典藏經典 115

絕望的刀刺進了我的青春：王爾德詩選 I
Selected Poems of Oscar Wilde: I

作　　者／王爾德 Oscar Wilde
繪　　者／奧伯利‧比亞茲萊 Aubrey Beardsley
譯　　者／張家綺
總 編 輯／鄧茵茵
文字編輯／王智群
內頁編排／廖勁智
行銷企畫／劉恩綺
發 行 所／好讀出版有限公司
　　　　　407 台中市西屯區工業 30 路 1 號
　　　　　407 台中市西屯區大有街 13 號（編輯部）
TEL: 04-23157795 FAX: 04-23144188 http://howdo.morningstar.com.tw
(如對本書編輯或內容有意見，請來電或上網告訴我們)
法律顧問／陳思成律師

總 經 銷／知己圖書股份有限公司
106 台北市大安區辛亥路一段 30 號 9 樓
TEL: 02-23672044 ／ 23672047 FAX: 02-23635741
407 台中市西屯區工業 30 路 1 號 1 樓
TEL: 04-23595819 FAX: 04-23595493
E-mail:service@morningstar.com.tw
網路書店：http://www.morningstar.com.tw
讀者專線：04-23595819#230
郵政劃撥：15060393（知己圖書股份有限公司）

印　　刷／上好印刷股份有限公司
初　　版／西元 2018 年 6 月 15 日
定　　價／ 200 元
如有破損或裝訂錯誤，請寄回台中市 407 工業區 30 路 1 號更換（好讀倉儲部收）

Published by How Do Publishing Co., Ltd.
2018 Printed in Taiwan
All rights reserved.
ISBN 978-986-178-457-1

讀者回函

只要寄回本回函，就能不定時收到晨星出版集團最新電子報及相關優惠活動訊息，並有機會參加抽獎，獲得贈書。因此有電子信箱的讀者，千萬別忘於寫上你的信箱地址

書名：**絕望的刀刺進了我的青春：王爾德詩選 I**

姓名：＿＿＿＿＿＿＿ 性別：□男 □女 生日：＿＿年＿＿月＿＿日

教育程度：＿＿＿＿＿＿＿＿＿

職業：□學生 □教師 □一般職員 □企業主管
　　　□家庭主婦 □自由業 □醫護 □軍警 □其他＿＿＿＿＿＿

電子郵件信箱（e-mail）：＿＿＿＿＿＿＿＿＿ 電話：＿＿＿＿＿＿

聯絡地址：□□□＿＿＿＿＿＿＿＿＿＿＿＿＿＿＿

你怎麼發現這本書的？

□書店 □網路書店（哪一個？）＿＿＿＿＿＿□朋友推薦 □學校選書
□報章雜誌報導 □其他＿＿＿＿＿＿＿＿＿

買這本書的原因是：＿＿＿＿＿＿＿＿＿＿＿

□內容題材深得我心 □價格便宜 □封面與內頁設計很優 □其他＿＿＿＿＿

你對這本書還有其他意見麼？請通通告訴我們：

＿＿＿＿＿＿＿＿＿＿＿＿＿＿＿＿＿＿＿

你買過幾本好讀的書？（不包括現在這一本）

□沒買過 □ 1～5 本 □ 6～10 本 □ 11～20 本 □太多了

你希望能如何得到更多好讀的出版訊息？

□常寄電子報 □網站常常更新 □常在報章雜誌上看到好讀新書消息
□我有更棒的想法＿＿＿＿＿＿＿＿＿＿

最後請推薦五個閱讀同好的姓名與 e-mail，讓他們也能收到好讀的近期書訊：

1. ＿＿＿＿＿＿＿＿＿＿＿＿＿＿＿＿
2. ＿＿＿＿＿＿＿＿＿＿＿＿＿＿＿＿
3. ＿＿＿＿＿＿＿＿＿＿＿＿＿＿＿＿
4. ＿＿＿＿＿＿＿＿＿＿＿＿＿＿＿＿
5. ＿＿＿＿＿＿＿＿＿＿＿＿＿＿＿＿

我們確實接收到你對好讀的心意了，再次感謝你抽空填寫這份回函

請有空時上網或來信與我們交換意見，好讀出版有限公司編輯部同仁感謝你！

好讀的部落格：http://howdo.morningstar.com.tw

好讀的臉書粉絲團：http://www.facebook.com/howdobooks

也可直接掃描
線上讀者回函

請填妥後對折黏貼，直接投郵即可，無須貼郵票。

廣告回函
臺灣中區郵政管理局
登記證第 3877 號
免貼郵票

好讀出版有限公司 編輯部收

407 臺中市西屯區何厝里大有街 13 號
電話：04-23157795-6　傳真：04-23144188

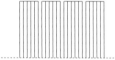

沿虛線對折

購買好讀出版書籍的方法：

一、先請你上晨星網路書店http://www.morningstar.com.tw檢索書目
　　或直接在網上購買

二、以郵政劃撥購書：帳號15060393　戶名：知己圖書股份有限公司
　　並在通信欄中註明你想買的書名與數量

三、大量訂購者可直接以客服專線洽詢，有專人為您服務：
　　客服專線：04-23595819轉230　傳真：04-23597123

四、客服信箱：service@morningstar.com.tw